MURDER ON THE JOB

We walked onto the loading dock. Some of the new employees seemed restless, and I wondered if they were considering making a break for it—I know I was.

"Ms. Randolph? You said we were supposed to be careful with the mannequins," Darlene said. "It doesn't look like everybody knew about that policy."

She pointed to two white legs sticking out from behind the Dumpster.

I got a weird feeling.

"Maybe the store needs another training class on the mannequins," Darlene said.

I went down the concrete steps and peered behind the Dumpster.

The legs didn't belong to a mannequin . . .

Books by Dorothy Howell

HANDBAGS AND HOMICIDE

PURSES AND POISON

SHOULDER BAGS AND SHOOTINGS

CLUTCHES AND CURSES

TOTE BAGS AND TOE TAGS

EVENING BAGS AND EXECUTIONS

BEACH BAGS AND BURGLARIES

SWAG BAGS AND SWINDLERS

POCKETBOOKS AND PISTOLS

Published by Kensington Publishing Corporation

Pocketbooks and Pistols

DOROTHY HOWELL

KENSINGTON BOOKS
http://www.kensingtonbooks.com

KENSINGTON BOOKS are published by

Kensington Publishing Corp.
119 West 40th Street
New York, NY 10018

All Kensington titles, imprints, and distributed lines are available at special quantity discounts for bulk purchases for sales promotion, premiums, fund-raising, educational, or institutional use.Special book excerpts or customized printings can also be created to fit specific needs. For details, write or phone the office of the Kensington Special Sales Manager: Attn. Special Sales Department. Kensington Publishing Corp., 119 West 40th Street, New York, NY 10018. Phone: 1-800-221-2647.

Kensington and the K logo Reg. U.S. Pat. & TM Off.

ISBN-13: 978-0-7582-9504-0
ISBN-10: 0-7582-9504-9
First Kensington Hardcover Edition: November 2016
First Kensington Mass Market Edition: March 2018

eISBN-13: 978-0-7582-9505-7
eISBN-10: 0-7582-9505-7
First Kensington Electronic Edition: November 2016

10 9 8 7 6 5 4 3 2 1

Printed in the United States of America

With love to Stacy, Judy, Brian, and Seth

ACKNOWLEDGMENTS

The author is extremely grateful for the love, support, and encouragement of many people. Some of them are: Stacy Howell, Judith Branstetter, Brian Branstetter, Seth Branstetter, Martha Cooper, and William F. Wu, PhD.

Many thanks to Evan Marshall of the Evan Marshall Agency, and John Scognamiglio and the talented team at Kensington Publishing for all their hard work.

Special thanks go out to Stacy Agner, Carol Beyner, Linda Herold, Sue Krekeler, Joyce Meyer, Bonnie Nothe, and Linda Rudesill.

Chapter 1

What was I thinking?

During my entire twenty-five years of life, I, Haley Randolph, with my it-makes-me-look-smart dark hair, my if-I'd-been-the-least-bit-interested-I-could-have-been-a-model five-foot-nine-inch height, and my not-nearly-enough-of-my-mom's-beauty-queen genes, had adopted certain codes of conduct to live by. They had served me well through many somebody-kill-me-now college classes and where-had-it-all-gone-so-wrong jobs. Only on rare occasions did I depart from these personal rules—and, honestly, I usually regretted it.

I sure as heck did this time.

"Have you got the paperwork? The forms? The checklist?" Rita asked.

We were in the why-do-customers-keep-buying-this-crappy-merchandise Holt's Department Store, where, in a moment of extreme desperation a year or so ago, I'd taken a job as a part-time salesclerk. Rita was the cashiers' supervisor.

I hate her.

"What about the welcome letter?" she asked. "Oh my God, you forgot the welcome letter, didn't you? I knew you'd forget the welcome letter."

She hates me back.

During a what-was-I-thinking moment here at Holt's a few weeks ago, I'd agreed to conduct the new-hire orientation. At the time, I'd been on a high over . . . something. I guess. I don't remember, exactly. But whatever it was, when I'd come to my senses and realized what I'd volunteered for, I was sure that when the time came to actually do the orientation, I could figure a way to wiggle out it.

Another bad decision on my part.

So here I was.

We were in the training room. Chairs were set up theater-style, awaiting the arrival of the new hires. On a table at the front of the room, I'd laid out the materials needed to conduct the orientation.

"Did you include the notice about the mannequins?" Rita asked, glaring at my sort-of neatly stacked forms. "None of those new hires better come to me about the mannequins."

Really, I double hate her.

"Did you read the new-hire orientation trainer's guide?" Rita asked.

There was a trainer's guide?

"What about the benefits handbooks?" Rita asked.

There was a handbook?

"I don't see the memo on the mannequins." Rita rifled through the forms. "You should know how important that memo is. You've worked here long enough to know this stuff."

Yes, I'd worked at Holt's for over a year, making me one of the store's most experienced employees—not something I put on my résumé.

I didn't need to since I already had an awesome job as an event planner at L.A. Affairs, a company that bent over backwards to satisfy every outrageous and idiotic whim of the rich and famous in Los Angeles and Hollywood. My schedule had lightened up considerably now that it was January. The holidays had been a blur for me as I'd planned and executed a number of this-year-it-will-be-perfect parties and family gatherings, and let's-drink-too-much-and-act-like-jackasses-while-we-can business events.

Okay, so you might wonder why, with my fabulous job at L.A. Affairs, I still subjected myself to the crappy working conditions, the hideous merchandise, and the management staff here at Holt's, who actually thought we sales clerks should knock ourselves out to do a great job for nine lousy bucks an hour.

Believe me, there was a good reason.

While my job at Holt's was nowhere near awesome, it did offer an if-this-is-a-dream-don't-wake-me employee discount at sister store Nuovo, a you-have-to-be-rich-to-shop-here boutique that sold the hottest, trendiest designer fashions and accessories. I wasn't rich, but with the eighty percent employee discount, I didn't have to be.

Reason enough to stay—for me, anyway.

We've all got our priorities.

"I know you're going to screw this up," Rita barked.

I'd had enough. Really, there was only so much I could take—especially from someone wearing stretch pants and a shirt with a bedazzled unicorn on the front.

"You don't know *anything*," I told her. "If you did, *you'd* have been asked to do the orientation. So move along. I have an orientation to conduct."

Rita's eyes narrowed until, I'm sure, she could hardly see.

"You'd better make certain these new hires are properly trained, Princess," she hissed. "And I'd better *not* get any questions from them about the mannequins."

I gave her stink eye right back until she finally whipped around and left.

A few minutes later, six newly hired sales clerks of various sizes, shapes, colors, and ages wandered into the training room. Some looked scared and overwhelmed, others eager and excited. One guy looked as if he'd been recently released.

Leave it to HR.

They took seats scattered across the dozen chairs. Several, who already seemed bored, plopped down on the back row and were, of course, likely to become my friends.

One girl took a chair front row, center. She wore her dark hair cut short and had on sensible pants, blouse, and shoes.

I knew she'd be trouble.

Her hand shot up.

There's always *one*.

"Darlene here, Darlene Phelps. Are we having CBT training today?" she asked.

CBT training? What the heck was that?

Maybe I should have read the trainer's guide.

This, however, was no time to admit it, so what could I do but channel my mom's former-beauty-queen posture—back slightly arched, shoulders squared, chin up—and say, "Everything will be covered throughout the orientation."

Darlene nodded as if I'd just divulged the nuclear missile launch codes, then grabbed a yellow legal-size tablet and pen from her tote bag and wrote something down.

I didn't remember much about my own new-hire orientation—I'd drifted off—so I began by handing out the lanyards with their official Holt's ID cards attached, then passed out the benefits handbook and the forms that had to be completed.

Darlene paged through the handbook, then raised her hand. "I have a question about our eligibility for profit sharing."

Holt's offered profit sharing?

"On page sixteen, it covers the options for profit sharing," Darlene said, then flipped ahead. "But contradictory information is on page thirty-six."

I didn't know what I was more surprised by—that Darlene had read the book that quickly, or that Holt's had enough benefits to fill up thirty-six pages.

"Please hold all your questions until the end," I announced.

Darlene made another note on her tablet, then asked, "Who is going to answer our questions? The store manager? Someone from corporate?"

The very *last* thing I wanted was someone from the Holt's corporate office in our store. My ex-official boyfriend was Ty Cameron, the fifth generation of driven, obsessive control freaks to run the family-owned Holt's chain of department stores. We'd broken up so I *knew* everyone at the corporate office was talking about me.

That's what I would have done.

I ignored Darlene's question and pushed ahead.

"I need everyone's IDs and Social Security cards," I told the group.

It was standard procedure for anyone starting a new job in California—and probably other places—to provide proof of citizenship, so all the new hires had been instructed to bring the items to orientation.

Everybody dug the cards out. I collected them and opened the door.

"Continue filling out the forms," I said. "I'll be back in a few minutes."

Darlene's hand went up again. I shot out the door and closed it behind me.

The photocopier was located in the store's assistant managers' office, and I'd intended to go straight there. Really. But the vending machines in the employee breakroom called out to me—I mean, jeez, I hadn't had anything chocolate in a while and my afternoon definitely needed a boost, so what else could I do?

The breakroom was equipped with a refrigerator, microwave, and vending machines. The walls were plastered with posters about upcoming Holt's sales events—as if anyone but upper management really cared—and info about our rights as employees. Hanging above the time clock was a clipboard with the daily work schedule. Along the back wall were lockers for our personal belongings. There was also a whiteboard that Rita gleefully used to write the names of anyone who reported late for a shift—five tardies in one month and you got fired. Two names were listed.

A few employees sat at the tables, flipping through our outdated selection of magazines and munching on snacks. I got a ten from my handbag—a mind-blowing Dolce & Gabbana satchel—and fed it into the vending machine. I started punching buttons and my cell phone vibrated in my pocket. The caller ID screen showed a message from Marcie, my best bestie. She'd sent me a link.

My adrenaline level shot up—and I hadn't even eaten any chocolate yet.

This had to be good.

Marcie and I had been friends forever. She and I shared a love—okay, really, it was an all-consuming, totally out-of-proportion, way-past-obsession love—of designer handbags.

I clicked on the link and there, before my eyes, materialized the most gorgeous handbag I'd seen in my entire life—and that's saying something. It was the Mystique, a blue leather clutch embellished with peacock feathers. My knees got weak just looking at it. I absolutely *had* to have it.

Immediately, I mentally put together the mission Marcie and I would undertake to find this much-sought-after bag—a grid-pattern, color-coded, north-south sweep of boutiques through Los Angeles, cross-referenced with online searches. We'd done this a bazillion times so—

Wait. Hang on. I didn't have to do this any longer.

I grabbed my Snickers bar and two packages of M&M's from the vending machine tray and sank into a chair. Marcie and I didn't have to comb the city and the Internet, and fight the crowds at the stores to find the Mystique. We didn't have to sweat it out on a waiting list. All I had to do was call Nuovo, tell them I wanted two of the bags, and they would put them aside until I leisurely strolled into their shop and picked them up.

It would be easy—but, somehow, kind of disappointing.

Weird, huh?

"You want to hear some b.s.?"

Bella walked into the breakroom. She was one of my Holt's BFFs. Mocha to my vanilla, she was about my age, tall, with a flair for hair styling. She intended to be a hairdresser to the stars and was working at Holt's to save for beauty school. In the meantime, she experimented with different looks on her own hair. I sensed she had some kind of geometric theme going because she'd fashioned her hair into the shape of a triangle atop her head.

"I mean, this is some real b.s.," Bella said.

I didn't bother commenting. She knew I always wanted to hear some b.s.

I ripped open a bag of M&M's and dumped most of it into my mouth.

"A customer just tried to take off with an armload of jeans," Bella said, feeding coins into the vending machine. "And get this—she had on flip-flops. Flip-flops. How's she going to make a run for her car in the parking lot in flip-flops? What's wrong with people? Why aren't they thinking ahead?"

"Did she get away?" I asked, and poured the rest of the M&M's into my mouth.

"Fell down," Bella said. She got her soda and dropped into the chair across the table from me. "Face-planted right in front of the doors. Busted her lip."

"She'll probably sue."

"If she had any sense, she would." Bella gestured to the stack of driver's licenses and Social Security cards on the table. "You're doing the orientation today?"

"Afraid so."

"Where's Lani? Why isn't she doing it?"

Lani was the woman who usually conducted the orientation.

"She was a no-show today," I said, and unwrapped my Snickers bar.

Bella shook her head. "There's something weird about her."

I couldn't disagree, which was why I was okay handling the orientation alone.

"Got any good-looking men in there?" Bella asked, nodding toward the training room down the hall.

"One guy looks like he should be institutionalized, and there's another one who might take first place in a serial killer look-alike contest," I said.

"Figures," Bella grumbled. "This place—"

"Ms. Randolph?"

Darlene appeared in the breakroom doorway. What the heck was she doing?

"The group has questions about the W-9," she told me, holding up the packet of forms I'd given the new hires to complete. "People are freaking out in there."

I was pretty sure Darlene was the only one freaking out.

"I'll be there in a minute," I told her.

Darlene hesitated, then finally left.

Bella rolled her eyes. "There's always one."

I finished my Snickers bar and dumped my trash, then stopped by the whiteboard. I looked at the names of the two employees who had been late for work that Rita had listed, erased them, and left the breakroom.

I headed down the hallway to the office shared by the store's assistant managers. Nobody was inside when I walked in. I spent a few minutes photocopying the documents, then put the copies in the file folder with Lani's name on it and returned to the training room.

The only person still working on the forms was Darlene. Everyone else was either chatting or on their phones; one guy was asleep.

"Time for the store tour," I announced as I handed back their cards.

Darlene waved her hand above her head. "I haven't finished my forms. I have questions."

Oh, crap.

She started asking me something and, really, I drifted off. Something nagged at my thoughts, something kind of important that I was supposed to do.

Then it hit me—the mannequins.

Holt's had recently purchased new mannequins on which to display our dismal array of so-called fashions. It seemed like a waste of money to me. I mean, really, you could drape the Holt's merchandise on blocks of solid gold and it still wouldn't make them desirable.

Every employee had been forced to endure a lengthy training session—complete with a PowerPoint presentation—given by somebody from corporate about the new mannequins. We had been harangued for two hours about how expensive they were, how delicate, how fragile, how only specially trained technicians were authorized to dress them.

The entire mind-numbing ordeal actually came down to two things—don't touch the mannequins and make sure the customers don't touch the mannequins. I could have conveyed the essence of the entire presentation with those two statements.

Really, why wasn't I running the entire world?

"Listen up," I announced to the group. "About the mannequins. Don't touch them. Okay?"

Everybody nodded—except, of course, for Darlene.

I was starting to not like Darlene.

"Is that a corporate policy?" she asked. "Or is it a store policy?"

Like it mattered?

"What if a customer can't find the size they want?" Darlene proposed. "What if the size they want is on the mannequin?"

"Don't touch the mannequins," I said.

"So, you're saying Holt's is willing to lose a sale?" she asked.

"The mannequins are new. The company paid a lot of money for them. Don't touch the mannequins," I told her.

I mean, jeez, how hard was that to understand?

"But what about providing good customer service?" Darlene asked. "The Holt's employee guidebook states on page three that we're to provide excellent customer service at all times. How is refusing to take something off of a mannequin providing good customer service?"

No way am I cut out for doing new-hire orientation

"Are we supposed to offend a paying customer *and* lose a sale?" Darlene asked.

I'm definitely going to have to figure a way to get out of doing this again.

"Are we?" She picked up her tablet and pen, ready to write something down.

Okay, now I really don't like Darlene.

"Well?" she asked.

I walked out of the room.

The new hires fell in behind me as I headed down the hallway.

"First, we're checking out the stockroom," I told them, then led the way through the double doors.

I loved the stockroom. Its massive shelving units were stuffed to capacity with fresh, new merchandise. It was usually quiet back here, unless the truck team was unloading, except for the store's canned music track that played quietly. Plus, it was a great place to hide out from customers.

I decided I'd let the new hires figure that out on their own.

I led the way through the shelving units, pointing and explaining as we passed the mannequin farm, the janitor's closet, and the returns area, then told them that the huge staircase led to the upper floor, where smaller, lighter merchandise was stored. Two of the girls were whispering, another was texting. Everyone else was paying attention. Darlene, for some reason, was making notes on her tablet.

"This is the loading dock," I said, doing my very best Vanna White hand gesture.

I hit a button and one of the big doors rose, groaning and clattering until it reached the top of its tracks. Outside, the afternoon sun shone in bright escape-now-while-you-can fashion, illuminating the building's rear parking lot, the

Dumpsters, and the backs of the other stores in the shopping center.

We walked out onto the loading dock. Some of the new employees seemed restless, and I wondered if they were considering making a break for it—I know I was.

"Ms. Randolph? You said we were supposed to be careful with the mannequins," Darlene said. "It doesn't look like everybody knew about that policy."

She pointed to two white legs sticking out from behind the Dumpster.

I got a weird feeling.

"Maybe the store needs another training class on the mannequins," Darlene said.

I went down the concrete steps and peered behind the Dumpster.

The legs didn't belong to a mannequin. They were attached to a girl.

She was dead.

Chapter 2

"How's the orientation going?" Bella asked.

"Not that great," I said.

I was in the breakroom eyeing the candy in the vending machine—which I desperately needed. Only a few minutes ago, I'd broken the news to Jeanette, the store manager, that I'd spotted a dead body behind the Dumpster. She wasn't happy—like it was my fault, or something. I'd left it up to her to make the phone calls. She knew the drill.

"You heard?" I asked Bella.

I figured she had—the only thing that moved through Holt's faster than a shoplifter was weapons-grade gossip.

Bella nodded. "The cops are out back doing their thing by now, huh?"

I'd only hung around long enough to make sure the victim was actually dead. It wasn't hard to figure out, thanks to that big yucky hole in the center of her chest.

"You ask me, I think—" Bella paused. "Where are all the new hires?"

Oh, crap. I'd sent them to the training room and forgotten about them.

I'm really not cut out for conducting orientation.

"Later," I said, and left the breakroom.

In the hallway, I could see that the door to Jeanette's office was closed. I figured she was on the phone with the corporate office, explaining what had happened.

I headed for the training room. Although I had hustled the new hires back into the stockroom right away, they'd seen the dead body. There was, of course, no way I could smooth that over. They were surely going to be upset.

I'm not good with upset people.

I was just going to have to wing it. I doubted there was a finding-a-dead-body-at-the-store chapter in the Holt's trainer's guide.

I paused at the door, drew in an I'm-going-to-do-this breath, and went into the training room. It was empty.

I went into semi-panic mode.

Where the heck was everyone? I'd specifically told them to stay here so they could be questioned by the police. Plus, they all had their official Holt's ID cards. Were they wandering willy-nilly through the store, wreaking havoc with the customers and merchandise?

Not that I really cared, but still.

Darlene popped up from a chair in the back corner.

"Where is everybody?" I asked.

"They quit."

Oh, crap.

Darlene hoisted her tote bag onto her shoulder and walked closer.

"They were freaked out," she told me.

Honestly, I couldn't blame them.

Darlene stopped in front of me and drew herself up taller. For a minute, I thought she might salute.

"But I'm staying," she told me. "I don't care what the others said about the store."

"Oh. Okay."

"Or you."

"*Me?*"

"Haley?"

Jeanette stood in the doorway looking none too happy. Really, I wasn't all that happy myself—but mostly because this was the second time today I'd been subjected to the dreadful outfit Jeanette had on.

As the store manager, she made big bucks and could easily afford on-trend clothes that were appropriate for her position. Instead, she dressed in outfits straight off the Holt's racks—most of which eventually ended up on the Holt's clearance racks.

I mean, really, our own who-cares-what-it-looks-like-it's-cheap customers wouldn't buy most of them—so what does that tell you?

Today, Jeanette had on a dress and bolero

jacket—not the best cut for a tall, plus-size gal—that featured swirls of yellow and orange on a gray background.

It looked like one of those avant-garde pieces that nobody wanted to admit really looked like a second-grader's art project.

"The detectives are in my office," Jeanette said. "They want to see you now."

Oh, crap.

I knew I'd have to talk to the cops sooner or later—although I'd hoped for later.

I headed out the door and down the hallway to her office, mentally reminding myself to remain calm—I don't really like being calm—and to say as little as possible no matter what the detectives said—I'm not really good at that, either.

Jeanette's office door stood open. I stepped inside and—oh my God, there sat Detective Madison. I'd had several run-ins with him during other homicide investigations.

He hates me.

He'd convinced himself that I was some sort of one-person crime wave always getting away with—well, murder.

"Look who's here," Detective Madison declared from his seat behind Jeanette's desk. "Isn't this a coincidence?"

I knew he wasn't talking about Jeanette, but I glanced back just in case. She'd disappeared. Great.

Madison was an old-school detective who should have retired a long time ago.

He was definitely past his best-by date.

He had a comb-over and a beach-ball belly. I

was pretty sure he had on that same sport coat and tie the last time I saw him.

Standing behind him and off to the right was his much younger, more handsome partner, Detective Shuman. He was early thirties with light brown hair and a guy-next-door look about him.

We'd gotten to know each other during several homicide investigations and some personal situations. Nothing romantic, but there was some sort of heat between us, which we managed to ignore since, for much of the time I'd known Shuman, I'd had an official boyfriend and he'd had an official girlfriend. I'm a stickler about that sort of thing.

"Darlene, here. Darlene Phelps."

She pushed herself in front of me.

What the heck was she doing in here?

Madison looked surprised, Shuman slightly concerned.

"My notes, sir." Darlene pulled her legal tablet from her tote bag and placed it on the desk in front of Madison. "I included a chronological timeline of the events of the afternoon."

She did *what?*

Detective Madison studied the tablet. Shuman peered over his shoulder.

Darlene leaned forward and flipped the page. "I also prepared a diagram of the crime scene."

She made a *what*?

"It's color coded," she said. "And it's to scale."

Jeez, talk about a suck-up.

"Why were you at the crime scene, Ms. Phelps?" Madison asked.

"New-hire orientation, sir," Darlene told him. "Tour of the premises conducted by Ms. Randolph."

Madison cut his gaze to me and smirked. "Oh, really? Ms. Randolph was in charge of the orientation? How'd she do with that?"

"Honestly, sir," Darlene said, "I don't think she really liked the assignment."

Oh my God, why did she say that?

It was true, of course, but why would she tell Madison? Didn't she know what homicide detectives did with that kind of info? Hadn't she ever watched a *Law & Order* rerun?

Madison shot me a cat-who-swallowed-the-canary grin. "So why do you think she was doing it? Maybe to get off the sales floor and have the run of the building unnoticed?"

Oh, crap.

I didn't need GPS to figure out where this was going.

"Possibly," Darlene agreed.

"During the orientation, was Ms. Randolph present the entire time?" Madison asked.

"No, sir," she told him. "She left the training room. Frankly, I had to go search for her."

"She was gone that long, was she?"

I could almost see Madison's mind working. He was twisting everything around, making it seem like I was guilty of murder.

"Why do you think Ms. Randolph took the new hires to the rear of the store to see the Dumpster?" Madison asked. "Maybe because she wanted one of the new hires to spot the body? So she wouldn't look guilty?"

"She didn't seem upset or panicked by the discovery." Darlene pointed to the tablet. "I noted that in my report."

Okay, now I officially hate Darlene.

"Well, thank you, Ms. Phelps. You've certainly added a great deal to our investigation," Detective Madison said, looking altogether pleased with himself and the situation.

"Glad to help, sir." Darlene left the office.

Shuman caught my eye. He looked worried. I was bordering on panic mode.

Several tense moments dragged by. Madison glared at me, apparently trying to force a confession by drilling me with cop stink eye. No way was I falling for that.

"You're pretty popular here at the store, wouldn't you say, Ms. Randolph?" Madison asked. "You're a long-time employee. Been here, what, over a year now, isn't it?"

I didn't respond. Madison was going somewhere with this, somewhere I knew I wouldn't like.

"You're well thought of, right?" he went on. "After all, you're doing the orientation. That's a step up, isn't it? So you know people, don't you? The other employees, I mean."

I got a yucky feeling.

"You must have known Asha McLean," Madison said.

My yucky feeling got yuckier.

"Did you know her?" Madison asked. "The murder victim. Asha McLean. She used to work here."

That was Asha's body I'd found?

Oh, crap.

Yes, I remembered Asha—barely. She was in her late twenties, with dark hair, and an average build. In fact, everything about her was average. She'd worked here for a few weeks during the Christmas season so we sort-of knew each other. I hadn't seen her since. No wonder I hadn't recognized her.

"You two didn't get along?" Madison asked. "You two had a disagreement? A fight?"

"That never happened."

"Maybe the two of you had some sort of business arrangement?" he asked. "Something on the illegal side?"

"I hardly knew her."

"She didn't come back to the store today looking for you?" he asked. "Trying to settle an old score, maybe? So you decided to strike first?"

"And what—I just happened to have a gun on me that I shot her with?" I demanded.

"Well? Did you?" Madison asked.

"No! No, of course not."

Madison grinned again, as if he were enjoying seeing me squirm—which, I'm sure, he was. I wasn't going to give him the satisfaction.

Channeling my pageant mom's I'm-better-than-you attitude, I said, "If you have further questions, Detective, you can talk to my lawyer."

I put my nose in the air, whipped around, and left the office. I'd only made it to the door of the employee breakroom when someone called my name. I looked back and saw Detective Shuman hurrying toward me.

"You have a lawyer?" he asked.

Of course I didn't have a lawyer. I only said that to—

Wait. Hang on.

I'd been kind-of dating a really hot guy for a while, an attorney I'd met through my job at L.A. Affairs.

"Yes, I have a lawyer," I said. "Sort of."

"Is he a criminal attorney?"

I wasn't sure. He'd told me, but I'd drifted off.

"Madison wishes I was guilty," I said. "I'm not."

Shuman shook his head. "He's got it in for you. You'd better take this seriously."

I didn't want to think Shuman was right, but I knew he was.

"Will you let me know what's happening with the investigation?" I asked.

Shuman hesitated. He couldn't compromise his job or his integrity. I knew that. But we'd worked together on cases in the past. And I was, after all, *me*.

"Look," I said. "All I'm asking is that you let me know as much as you can."

Shuman still didn't say anything.

I nodded toward the sales floor. "Somebody here probably knows something. I'll see what I can find out and pass it on."

He hesitated another few seconds, then nodded. "I'll keep you in the loop as much as possible."

"Cool. Thanks."

Shuman nodded and headed back into the office.

Oh my God, what a day I was having. I was upset and weirded out, big time. I had a little headache going.

So what could I do but go shopping for a new handbag?

Chapter 3

Nuovo had a shop near the mall in Valencia, just a few minutes' drive from the Holt's store and my apartment. I'd run by my place after my shift ended and changed into something I actually wanted to be seen in—a skirt, sweater, and boots—and freshened my makeup and hair. Marcie and I had agreed to meet at Nuovo, then have dinner and catch up.

The mall was a good mix of upscale and mid-range stores. I shopped here often. An outside plaza opened at one end of the mall and gave way to several blocks of trendy shops, boutiques, art galleries, candy stores, a movie theater, office buildings, and restaurants. The narrow streets and wide sidewalks urged shoppers to stroll while oversized display windows invited them inside.

I nosed in at the curb and sent Marcie a text message telling her I'd arrived. I didn't get a response right away, so I figured that meant she was driving and would be here shortly.

I could have waited in my Honda, but I got out. I'd just bought these killer boots and, really, people should have the opportunity to see me in them. I've got my mom's long pageant legs—the only thing I inherited from her, as she often pointed out—so my short skirt was working for me, too.

I strolled down the sidewalk, keeping my cell phone close for when I heard from Marcie. The trees and shrubs twinkled with tiny lights, and a sound system played a song that seemed vaguely familiar. The shop windows were lit, displaying a tempting variety of credit-card-busting must-haves.

Thoughts of my ex-official boyfriend exploded in my head, as they always did when I shopped here. In addition to running the Holt's chain and Holt's International, Ty had opened Wallace, a boutique he'd named after some ancient ancestor, across the street. Down the block was the restaurant where we'd had our first sort-of date.

Ty was tall, with light brown hair, deep blue eyes, and an athletic build. He was super smart, of course. We'd dated for a long time, but his commitment to Holt's and the five generations of the family-owned business he had on his back made things tough—for me, anyway. Ty had told me right from the start that the family business would come first. He'd kept his word. Finally, we'd decided we just couldn't make it work—no, really, Ty had decided and we'd broken up.

I glanced at my cell phone. Still no word from Marcie. I wished she'd hurry up. As my BFF, she had a way of keeping me from venturing back into breakup zombieland, the place I'd called home for a long time after Ty and I called it quits—the place that tugged at me right now.

How could it not?

The last time I'd seen Ty was a few months ago. He'd been through a rough patch. In a move totally unlike him, he'd taken a leave of absence from Holt's, bought a cherry-red convertible Ferrari Spider, and hit the road.

I stared across the street at the outdoor seating area of the restaurant where we'd sat on our first kind-of date. Ty, so handsome. Generous to a fault. Kind, caring. He was everything I wanted in a boyfriend—except for his inability to commit to me and put our relationship first in his life.

But he'd sort of done that, I reminded myself. A few months ago, that last time I'd seen him, he'd come to the Holt's store in the Ferrari and told me he was going away for a while. He'd asked me to come with him.

My heart still fluttered at the recollection.

He'd been through a lot, and I could tell he was questioning most everything about his life. He needed time to figure things out, and I knew he could only do that alone.

I'd told him no. I didn't go with him that day.

I hadn't heard from him since.

Heaviness settled around me, and it would have been easy—welcome, almost—to slip back into the zombie-like state I'd existed in after our breakup.

But I couldn't allow myself to go through that again.

So what could I do but think about murder?

I turned away from Wallace and the restaurant, and headed the other way down the sidewalk.

Asha McLean had been murdered, shot in the chest, behind the Holt's store. What was she doing back there?

Aside from delivery trucks and the trash collectors, the only things that should have been back there were employees parking their cars. But Asha didn't work for Holt's. If she had been at the store shopping, why wouldn't she have parked out front?

It occurred to me that maybe Asha had gone to work at one of the stores that adjoined Holt's in the shopping center. But if that were true, why would she be behind Holt's and not the store at which she was employed?

Detective Madison had suggested something illegal was going on with Asha. Maybe he knew something or maybe he was just fishing, trying to get info out of me. At this point, I had no way of knowing.

She could have been having a smoke or meeting someone. A boyfriend, maybe? I had no clue.

She'd worked at Holt's as a sales clerk during

the Christmas rush. Honestly, I barely remembered her. The store had been the usual holiday mad house of cranky customers, screaming kids, and long hours. I couldn't even say with any certainty when Asha was hired or when she quit.

The only thing I knew about her for sure was that Detective Madison was trying hard to pin her death on me.

I checked my cell phone. Marcie still hadn't texted me. She worked at a bank in downtown Los Angeles and was probably inching her way through rush-hour traffic.

I'd promised I'd wait for her to check on the Mystique at Nuovo, but I couldn't stand around any longer. My evening definitely needed a boost. She'd understand. That's what BFFs did.

A chime pealed when I stepped inside Nuovo. The shop had pale hardwood floors, chrome fixtures, and track lighting—very contemporary. The sales clerks were all about my age, tall, thin, with full-on makeup, dark hair pulled back in a low bun, and short, black dresses.

They looked like they were all members of some ultra-cool cult.

I mean that in the nicest way, of course.

The fashions here were beyond phenomenal. Racks of designer dresses, skirts, blouses, and coats, and shelves that held sweaters, jeans, and—handbags. Lots of handbags. Gorgeous handbags.

This was, I'm sure, what heaven looked like.

"Good evening, Ms. Randolph," a sales clerk said as she walked over. "May I assist you?"

Wow, was this awesome service, or what? I'd

only been in here a few times, but all the clerks remembered my name.

On occasions such as this, I couldn't help channeling my mom's sedate, sophisticated perhaps-I-will-allow-you-to-wait-on-me look—it must be genetic—and said, "I'm interested in a Mystique bag."

Yes, I actually said that quietly when what I wanted to do was rip through the stockroom and find it myself.

"An excellent choice," the clerk replied, smiling and nodding her approval. "Do you have a personal shopper with us, Ms. Randolph?"

During my previous visits here, no one had mentioned a personal shopper. This must be something new—which I was totally on board with.

"No, I don't."

"Then please allow me to assist you," she said. "My name is Chandra."

I gestured to the handbags on display—Gucci, Dior, Gucci, Prada, all the best designers—and said, "Do you have the Mystique available this evening?"

"I'm so very sorry, Ms. Randolph. The Mystique isn't in stock yet. We're waiting to receive our first shipment, and are anxious to see the bag ourselves. The demand is so great, the designer can't keep up," Chandra said. "I hope you'll accept my apology that we're not able to provide you with one this evening."

How could anybody be that nice?

Maybe she was really a robot.

"If you'll allow me," Chandra said, "I would be pleased to order one for you."

She wouldn't last ten minutes working at Holt's.

"Thank you," I said. "I'll need two of them."

"Of course. Would you kindly walk this way?"

She led me to the cash register at the rear of the store and tapped the keys for a few seconds, then nodded.

"Your bags will arrive in a few days," she said. "Shall I text you when they arrive?"

"Please do," I said.

She hit a couple more keys, then said, "May I assist you in any other way?"

A zillion things flew into my head—I was a sort-of suspect in a murder, my ex-official boyfriend hadn't contacted me in months, there wasn't enough work at L.A. Affairs to keep me busy so I had to spend time at Holt's—but she couldn't help me with any of those things. I thanked her and left the store.

Just as I stepped outside, I spotted Marcie's car swinging into a parking space. She jumped out and walked over.

"My phone died," she told me, "and I forgot my charger this morning."

Marcie was petite and blond—my polar opposite—and loved fashion as much as I did. She had on a fabulous pencil skirt and sweater that were really working for her.

"You got new boots?" she asked.

"They're kind of slutty."

"I know. I love them."

I nodded toward Nuovo. "I ordered Mystiques for us. They'll be here soon."

"Awesome," Marcie said. "Dinner?"

"As long as we start with drinks," I said, which, really, wasn't like me. I'm a real old lady when it comes to drinking and driving.

"It's been that kind of a day, huh?" Marcie asked.

"Like you wouldn't believe."

We walked down the block to a little bistro and got a table outside. Nights in Southern California, even January nights, were seldom cold, but there was a fire pit and several heaters going, making it comfy. Most of the tables were filled. Conversation was subdued.

We ordered wine and dinner, then got right into it.

"Okay, what's going on?" Marcie asked.

"I found somebody murdered at Holt's today."

"You did?" Marcie didn't seem surprised. She'd been through this with me before. "I hadn't heard."

The Holt's publicity department had lots of practice keeping this sort of thing quiet—finally, something corporate did right.

"And you'll never guess who caught the case," I said.

"Oh, no." Marcie shook her head. "Not Madison."

"He's already gunning for me."

The waiter served our wine. I took a big sip.

"Shuman promised to keep me up to speed

on the investigation," I said. "I'll see what I can find out at the store."

"Aren't you working at L.A. Affairs this week?"

"I don't really have much going on there. Nobody does, at this time of year," I said.

"What about Valentine's Day?"

I drank more wine. "No way. I told them I'm not planning any Valentine's Day parties."

"So you'll be free that night. Cool." Marcie smiled. "Does this mean you'll be hosting your own, shall we say, private party?"

"I've thought about it," I said and emptied my glass. "How could I not? I mean, he's got to come back *sometime*. Maybe he has a big surprise reunion planned for us? A romantic evening or maybe a weekend? Valentine's Day would be the perfect time, right?"

Marcie stared at me for a minute then said, "You're talking about Ty, aren't you?"

"Well, yes."

"I'm talking about Liam. Liam Douglas. Remember him? The totally hot guy you've been dating?" Marcie demanded.

Oh my God, she was right.

"And you're talking about Ty, the guy who always put you second, broke up with you, then left town and hasn't contacted you once," Marcie said.

She sounded slightly annoyed and put out with me—and really, I couldn't blame her.

"For all you know, Ty is already back in town and hasn't bothered to call you," she said.

Okay, that kind of hurt.

But Marcie was right. Marcie was almost always right.

She'd been with me through my breakup with Ty and had helped me get over what had happened, and move on. I'd been a mess, and I could see why she didn't want me backsliding.

"Is this why you've been holding back with Liam?" Marcie asked. She gave me a pointed look. "You know you've been doing that."

She was right—again.

Liam and I had been dating for a while. We were past the I-have-to-eat-a-salad-at-dinner-so-I-don't-look-like-a-pig phase of our relationship, but we hadn't gone much further than that.

The waiter stopped at our table and served our dinner. I ordered another glass of wine.

"Did you see any other fabulous handbags at Nuovo?" Marcie asked.

I was relieved she'd changed the subject. We chatted for a while, made plans for claiming our Mystique bags when they arrived, and finished our meals.

"I'd better go," Marcie said. "There's a big meeting first thing in the morning. I can't be late."

"I have a shift at Holt's tomorrow," I said.

We paid our tab and walked back to our cars. I waved good-bye to Marcie as I got into my Honda. She drove away, but I couldn't seem muster the strength to put my key in the ignition.

Thoughts of Ty, Liam, Asha, Detective Madison, and Holt's raged in my head. I was mega-stressed.

No way could I go home. All I would do there was sit and stress myself out even further. I thought about calling Liam—he was, after all, my sort-of boyfriend—but we hadn't reached a point where I felt I could turn to him for comfort. Maybe I could go shopping. Or maybe I could—

Somebody tapped on my window. I jumped, then saw Jack Bishop leaning down, looking in at me.

Oh my God—*oh my God.* Jack Bishop.

Jack was simultaneously the hottest—and the coolest—guy on the entire planet. He was a private investigator, and as if that weren't fabulous enough, he was gorgeous, with a great build, dark hair, and eyes almost too beautiful for a man.

We'd met when I'd worked for a law firm downtown where he did some consulting. Jack was wired into almost everything. We'd worked together on some cases but hadn't gotten personally involved because of that whole I-have-an-official-boyfriend thing.

He opened my door and I got out.

Wow, he smelled great.

"Meeting someone?" he asked.

"Marcie. She just left," I explained. "What about you?"

Jack nodded down the block. "I met with a new client."

We looked at each other for a few seconds, then Jack said, "How about a drink?"

I'd already had two glasses of wine, and one was my limit when I was driving.

But one more glass of wine couldn't hurt anything.

Could it?

Chapter 4

What the heck?

My eyes opened to tiny slits. They felt scratchy. My mouth tasted yucky, and jeez, my head was hurting. What was wrong with me?

I forced both eyes open and—

Where was I?

I sat straight up in bed—oh my God, I was in bed?

I went into semi-panic mode as I looked around.

This wasn't my bed. It wasn't my room.

And whose T-shirt was I wearing?

I sprang up, hurried to the window, and cracked the plantation shutters a tiny fraction. Morning sunlight beamed in, nearly blinding me. I squinted and saw a parking lot one floor below, and realized I was in an apartment or maybe a condo complex. But whose?

My phone was on the nightstand. I grabbed it

and saw I had one missed call. It had come in late last night from Liam.

I looked around the room—gray sheets, dark wood furniture, decorator-selected art on the walls—and knew it was definitely a man's room.

Liam's room?

My brain refused to process any information, but I forced myself to think.

No, I hadn't seen Liam last night. At least, I didn't remember seeing Liam last night. The last thing I clearly remembered was meeting up with Jack and—

Oh my God. *Oh my God.*

Was I in Jack's bedroom?

Had I spent the night *here*? With *him*?

I crept to the bedroom door and opened it a crack. All I could see was a hallway, the doors to another bedroom and a bathroom, and a staircase leading downstairs. I saw no one. I heard nothing.

Should I call Jack's name? No, wait. What if I really was at Liam's?

Would that be totally awkward, or what?

Okay, this was more than I could handle.

I dashed around the bedroom, threw on my clothes, and grabbed my cell phone. As I was envisioning calling Marcie to pick me up, I rushed down the stairs and spotted my handbag and keys on a table by the front door. Next to them was a stack of mail. The Edison bill on top was addressed to Jack.

Oh my God, what had I done last night?

I ramped up to total panic mode.

Squeezing my eyes shut, I forced my thoughts

back to last night. The restaurant. Having another glass of wine. Talking to Jack about the murder at Holt's. Having another glass of wine. Telling him about the Mystique clutch. Having another glass of wine. Telling him about . . . about—oh my God, I couldn't remember what else I'd talked to Jack about. I couldn't remember what had happened after that.

My eyes popped open.

Jack must have brought me here. Had I passed out? Was my mouth gaping open? Was I snoring? Drooling?

The cringe-worthy image sent a shudder through me.

No way did I want to see Jack right now. Not when I couldn't remember exactly what had happened. Not when I was at this much of a disadvantage.

I grabbed my things, went outside and followed the sidewalk to a parking lot. I hit the button on my remote, my car chirped, and I spotted it at the end of the row.

I had no idea how it had gotten here.

I *really* hoped I hadn't driven it.

I jumped in and sped away.

"I knew you'd screw up the orientation, Princess," Rita barked as I walked into the Holt's employee breakroom.

After the morning I'd had, Holt's, orientation, and Rita—most especially Rita—were the last things I was concerned about.

Leaving Jack's place—oh my God, I still

couldn't believe that had happened—I'd swung through Starbucks, which I desperately needed, and chugged my all-time favorite drink, a mocha Frappuccino. I'd gone to my apartment and pulled myself together, and had managed to get to Holt's on time.

I still didn't feel all that great—despite the Frappie.

This thing with Rita wasn't helping.

About a half-dozen other employees were scattered around the breakroom, some eating, others chatting, all of them wishing they were anywhere but here.

Or maybe that was just me.

"Because of you, almost all the new hires quit," Rita said.

I walked past her and stowed my handbag—a Dooney & Bourke barrel that far surpassed my Holt's-worthy jeans and navy-blue sweater—in my locker. I palmed my cell phone—we're not supposed to have them with us on the sales floor, but oh well—and saw a text from Juanita.

Crap.

How much worse was this day going to get?

Juanita was my mom's housekeeper. She'd been with our family for as long as I could remember.

I ignored the text and slid my cell phone into the pocket of my jeans.

"Now what are we supposed to do?" Rita demanded, as I headed for the time clock. "We're short-staffed."

Some of the employees seated at the tables glanced at me.

"Everybody is going to have to work longer hours," she said.

A murmur went through the room.

"Everybody is going to have to cover more shifts," Rita went on. "Days off and vacations will be cancelled."

Now everyone was staring.

"All because you screwed up the orientation," Rita told me.

The unpleasant murmur morphed into grumbling, and I was hit with major stink-eye from everyone.

"You'd better hope the rumor I heard isn't true," Rita said.

Rumor? What rumor?

I hate it when I miss a rumor.

A guy I didn't know got up from a table. "Yeah, thanks a lot, Haley."

Two girls rose, gave me serious bitch face, and followed him out of the breakroom.

Rita glared at me for a few more seconds, then left.

Oh my God, what was going on?

In a complete departure from my own personal code of conduct, I clocked in three minutes early and went out onto the sales floor. The store was crowded, thanks to Holt's yes-Christmas-is-over-but-that's-no-reason-not-to-continue-running-up-your-credit-card January sales.

I made my way past the children's clothing department to the housewares section. I spotted Bella unloading towels from a U-boat. Today she'd fashioned her hair into a number of disks that spanned her head.

She looked like a radar installation.

Standing next to her was Sandy, my other Holt's BFF.

Sandy was young with hair that varied between red and blond, which she usually wore in a ponytail. She always managed to find the best in any situation—which was really annoying at times—including her tattoo artist boyfriend who treated her like crap. Despite my oh-so-good advice, she refused to break up with him.

Go figure.

"Everybody's talking about what happened yesterday," Sandy said, as she arranged washcloths on a display shelf. "Poor Asha."

Here was the boost my day desperately needed. Maybe I could learn something that would lead me to Asha's murderer and get me out of Detectives Madison's crosshairs.

"You knew Asha?" I asked.

"She was nice," Sandy said.

"I thought she was weird," Bella told me, and wedged a stack of towels onto a shelf.

"She was so interested in everything that went on in the store," Sandy said. "She loved it here."

"See? Weird," Bella said.

I couldn't disagree.

"She wanted to know all about where the stock came from, who kept track of the inventory, what happened to the merchandise that didn't sell," Sandy said. "It seemed like she wanted to seriously work here. Seriously."

Bella and I exchanged an eye roll.

"So why did she quit?" I asked.

"Maybe she came to her senses," Bella said.

"No, no, I don't think that was it," Sandy said, and lapsed into thought for a few seconds. "She got a better-paying job, I think. Yeah, that was it. She really needed the money."

"Remember that old beat-up Chevy she drove?" Bella said.

The thing was a real eyesore, with a bashed-in door, a dent in the rear bumper, and a primer-gray fender. You couldn't miss it in the parking lot.

"Any idea why she was here yesterday, hanging around out back?" I asked.

"No clue," Bella said, and picked up more towels from the U-boat. "You ask me, it's all b.s. Nobody's ever going to see me hanging around this place after I quit. That would be b.s. Serious b.s."

Sandy shrugged and said, "I can't believe Asha's really dead. It's so sad."

"And I can't believe they'd close the store because of her," Bella said.

My senses jumped to high alert.

"That's the rumor going around?" I asked.

"Yeah," Bella said. "What's supposed to happen to all of us?"

"Holt's has a lot of stores," Sandy said. "They can transfer us."

"After they work us half to death because we're shorthanded," Bella said. "They might even cancel my vacay. Now that's some b.s. right there."

"Everybody is blaming me for the new hires quitting," I said. "It wasn't my fault."

"Well, Haley, you did find the dead body," Sandy pointed out.

That made perfect sense so, of course, no way did I want to hang around and deal with it.

"Later," I said, and headed back across the store.

I'd been in such a rush to get out of the breakroom earlier, I hadn't checked the schedule to see which department I was assigned to work in. But when I reached the breakroom, I didn't go inside. I decided to talk to Jeanette and see if I could get more intel on the store-closing rumor.

My cell phone vibrated in my pocket as I headed down the hallway. Liam flew into my head. He'd called me last night.

I cringed at the memory. Liam was my sort-of boyfriend. Not only had I not returned his call last night, I'd . . . I'd—

Well, I'd done something. I didn't know what, exactly, which was why I never drank to excess. If I did something crazy or wild, I wanted to remember it, not be shocked when the pics showed up on Facebook.

I checked my phone's ID screen and saw another text message from Mom's housekeeper, Juanita. This was really strange. It had been a really strange morning. I wasn't all that happy about adding my mom to the mix.

Mom was a former pageant queen. In fact, she still thought she was a pageant queen. Everything in her life revolved around fashion, beauty, appearance, and, of course, herself. She was stunningly beautiful and completely out of touch with reality.

I'm not like that.

Growing up was a real joy.

Juanita's text indicated I should call because something was wrong. I wasn't alarmed. Mom's problems ranged from booking an emergency manicure after spotting a hangnail to requiring a therapy session because her issue of *Vogue* had arrived with a wrinkle in the cover.

No way was I calling her now.

When I walked into Jeanette's office, I thought I was on the verge of fainting, then realized the spots appearing before my eyes were actually on the purple and white polka-dot shirtwaist dress she was wearing.

Not a good look for her.

"Is the rumor true?" I asked as I walked inside.

Yeah, sure, Jeanette was the store manager and I was a lowly sales clerk, but Jeanette knew I'd been dating Ty, her boss. This obligated her to cut me some extra slack. She must have learned that Ty and I had broken up, but so far she hadn't treated me in a fashion commensurate with my position. I figured she was reluctant to do so, in case Ty and I got back together.

Really, you can't blame her.

"Corporate wants to get out in front of this situation and resolve the matter before it becomes a big news story," Jeanette explained.

If the store were already closed, even something as salacious as finding a murder victim on the premises would lose most of its punch, leaving little to report on. I could see why corporate thought this was a good idea—except for one thing.

"What about the employees?" I asked—and

our employee discount, I wanted to add. I didn't. It might make me seem shallow. Which, I guess, I was. But, oh my God, this involved an eighty percent discount on the fabulous Mystique clutch bag. How could I *not* be concerned?

"We'll be transferred to other Holt's stores, right?" I asked.

Jeanette's expression turned grim—not a good sign.

"Sales are down this month, as usual for January," she said. "There are a few openings in other stores. Not many."

This was really not a good sign.

"So who will get transferred to the open spots?" I asked, thinking, *And keep the employee discount at Nuovo, of course.*

"Employees selected for transfer will be those who have achieved our Employee of the Month award," Jeanette said.

What?

"The store will present one final award this month," Jeanette explained. "Whoever earns it will be assured of a place in another of our Holt's locations."

I went into serious panic mode.

To keep my job—and my employee discount at Nuovo—I was going to have to be the Employee of the Month?

Oh, crap.

Chapter 5

Oddly enough, I'd never been the Employee of the Month. I had no idea what the requirements were, but I knew I should find out.

I left Jeanette's office and stopped at the customer service booth. I'd often been assigned to this area of retail purgatory where we handled returns, did price adjustments, gave out gift boxes, and pretended to listen—maybe that was just me—to customers' complaints.

Grace was inside tapping on the keyboard of the inventory computer, putting a pile of returned sweaters back into the store's stock. I liked Grace. She was cool to work with—and that's saying something here at Holt's. She was young, petite, and always wore her hair in the trendiest styles. Just a week ago, she'd shaved one side of her head, left the rest of it short and spikey, and dyed it blue. It was really working for her.

"What do you know about becoming the Employee of the Month?" I asked when she walked over.

"Not much, since I'm marooned in this booth," she said. "There are sales goals and something about attendance, I think, that sort of thing. The info is in the employee benefits handbook."

Was I the only person who didn't know there was an employee benefits handbook?

Apparently.

Rita walked up. "You're supposed to be in the shoes department," she barked.

"I'm picking up go-backs," I told her.

It was a total lie, but so what?

Grace grabbed two boxes of shoes she'd rung back into the store's inventory and handed them to me. Is she cool or what?

Rita glared at me. I glared back as I walked away.

At least now I knew where I supposed to work today.

Hours that I was never going to get back passed as I stocked shelves, straightened up the department, and avoided waiting on all but two customers—a personal best for me. When my shift was close to ending—well, kind of close—I headed for the time clock.

The fabulous Mystique clutch had filled my head most of the afternoon. I absolutely had to have it, and the only way to get it—with an equally fabulous eighty percent discount—was to guarantee my continued employment with Holt's and qualify for a transfer by winning the Employee of the Month award. I figured it might be a bit of a stretch for me, but I was confident I could handle it. I can rise to most any occasion when I have to. Really.

I bypassed the breakroom and went into the assistant store managers' office. No one was there—whichever assistant manager was on duty was probably on the sales floor—so I went through the cabinet where the materials for the new-hire orientation were stored and grabbed an employee benefits handbook.

My cell phone vibrated in my pocket. I checked the ID screen and saw another text message from Juanita, asking me again to call my mom. I'd intended to call her after my shift ended—really, I swear—so I accessed my contact list.

But I couldn't quite bring myself to hit the button. Instead, I called Detective Shuman. With any luck, he and Madison had uncovered enough evidence to know I wasn't involved with Asha's death, making it easier for me to focus on whatever problem my mom was having.

"Please tell me you solved the murder," I said when he answered.

Shuman chuckled. "And get you off the hook this quickly? Forget it. Madison is going to drag this out as long as possible."

He'd said it in a joking way, but I was afraid he was right.

"That crackerjack partner of yours must have come up with all kinds of evidence by now," I said. "Anything you're willing to share?"

"Preliminary autopsy report indicates the victim was shot point-blank in the chest. A handgun. Thirty-eight," Shuman said. "This was up close and personal. A murder. No question about it."

"Any suspects?" I asked.

"Besides you?" Shuman chuckled again. "No, we're still gathering evidence."

He seemed to be in an awfully good mood for a homicide detective who was on duty. I guess some days were easier than others.

"What about Asha's car?" I asked.

I hadn't noticed Asha's banged-up Chevy in the parking lot when I'd discovered her body. It was impossible to miss, but with everything that was happening at that moment, I hadn't thought to look for it.

"We towed it in," Shuman said. "The lab guys are going over it."

He'd been so forthcoming, I wished I had some meaningful info to share. I went with what I had.

"I heard Asha quit Holt's because she got a higher-paying job someplace else. She needed money," I said. "Maybe she was involved with something illegal and that's what got her killed."

"Always a possibility," Shuman agreed.

He didn't say anything else so I figured that was all I was going to get from him today.

"Thanks for the update," I said. "I'm asking questions. I'll let you know if I hear anything else."

"Not a good idea, Haley."

Shuman switched to his cop voice. It was way hot, of course, but right now kind of frightening.

"Madison thinks you've involved somehow.

You should stay as far away from this as you can," he told me.

I didn't say anything. I wouldn't lie to Shuman, so I kept my mouth shut.

"I know you're not going to do that," he said. "Just be careful."

"That I can do," I said, and we ended the call.

I was about to access Juanita's latest text message when the image of Liam flew into my head.

Oh, crap.

Liam was my sort-of boyfriend. I should have called him first.

Maybe I need to work on my sort-of girlfriend skills.

I accessed my contacts list while I paced across the office, and called Liam. His voicemail picked up so I left an aren't-I-clever message.

Then Jack Bishop sprang into my thoughts and I realized he hadn't called me today. I was more than a little relieved. I still wasn't clear on exactly what had gone on last night, and no way did I want to face him until I remembered.

Since I was still on company time, I checked my texts and read Juanita's message. This one was worded a little stronger, insisting that I call right away.

Okay, now I was kind of worried. Juanita seldom contacted me, but she'd reached out several times today. Maybe something terrible really had happened to Mom.

I called my parents' house. Juanita answered right away.

"You have to come. Now," she said before I could ask anything.

Juanita sounded mega-stressed, which, of course, caused me to be mega-stressed.

"Your mother is terribly upset."

The possible death of a family member or close friend popped into my head.

"What happened?" I asked.

"I don't know," Juanita said. "She won't tell me."

Or maybe it was a medical problem. Troubling test results or bad lab reports. Something she could only tell me, her oldest daughter.

"Her copy of *Harper's Bazaar* magazine came two days ago," Juanita said. "She hasn't opened it yet."

Oh my God, it was worse than I thought.

"I'll be right there."

I grew up in a small mansion in La Cañada Flintridge, a town near Pasadena that was set against the San Gabriel Mountains overlooking the Los Angeles basin, with my older brother, now a pilot in the Air Force, and my younger sister, who attended UCLA and worked as a model. Dad was an aerospace engineer.

My folks still lived there. The place had been left to my mother, along with a trust fund, by her grandmother. Just how my great-grandma—long dead before I came along—had acquired such wealth was a generations-old family secret.

Mom had wanted me, her first-born daughter, to follow in her footsteps down the runway to beauty queen fame. I'd endured years of dance, modeling, singing, and nearly every other imaginable lessons—with Mom coaching me while she struggled to find some tiny kernel of actual talent in me.

Since I carried only fifty percent of her beauty queen genes—and most of them were recessive—things hadn't gone well. It didn't help that I hadn't really liked any of that stuff. Mom finally admitted defeat when, at age nine, I set the den curtains ablaze attempting to twirl fire batons.

By then, my younger sister, a nearly perfect genetic copy of our mother, began to display great promise in filling Mom's five-inch pumps. So that was that. She was in. I was out.

When I'd left Holt's, I'd hit the Starbucks drive-through and gulped down a Frappuccino, fortifying myself for whatever the heck was going on with Mom, and headed east on the 210. By the time I took the exit, my chocolate-coffee-caffeine-infused brain had conjured up every possible horrific thing that could have befallen Mom.

I drove up the winding road and pulled to a stop in the circular driveway, relieved that the house was still standing and the worst-case scenario I'd imagined—a serial bomber bent on destroying the homes of former beauty pageant winners—hadn't happened. Juanita must have been watching for me because she opened the front door before I even got out of the car.

"She's in the media room," she said, waving me toward the rear of the house with both hands, like a ground crew member marshaling a passenger jet away from the terminal.

I walked deeper into the house, to the spot Mom had recently redecorated and dubbed the media room, a large space with a giant TV, comfy recliners and sofas, and a crank-it-up-even-if-it-makes-us-deaf sound system. She'd finished the room off with framed posters of classic movies and TV shows, and artistically rendered film reels, cameras, and whatever you called those black and white boards they snapped before a scene was shot.

The TV was off, the lights were low, the room was silent.

I didn't know why Mom was in that particular room. I doubted it was to catch up on the news.

She was holding a glass of wine and staring at a *Back to the Future* movie poster. My mom was tall—like me—with dark hair—like me—and stunning beautiful—totally unlike me; I was merely pretty, as I'd overheard her say many times.

She was dressed in a Zac Posen sheath, four-inch Lou-boutins, perfectly coordinated accessories, with full-on hair and makeup—just your average housewife at home on a weekday afternoon.

"Mom?"

A few seconds passed before she turned away from Marty McFly and the DeLorean, and spotted me. Immediately, she straightened into her pageant stance and her well-practiced I'm-so-pleased-to-see-you expression—wide eyes, smile with narrowly parted lips, head tilted slightly to the left.

"Haley, what a nice surprise," she said. "I wasn't expecting anyone."

Mom seemed normal. She looked and sounded as she most always did. I couldn't imagine why Juanita had thought something was terribly wrong—despite Mom's avoidance of her newly arrived *Harper's Bazaar* magazine.

I was slightly miffed that I'd been so worried and rushed over here, apparently for nothing.

"So what's up?" I asked.

"Nothing," Mom insisted, and gestured with her wineglass. "I was just wandering through the house."

Note—she hadn't wandered into the utility closet and grabbed a mop to help Juanita scrub the floors.

"And I ended up in here . . . somehow," Mom said, looking around as if seeing the room for the first time.

Okay, that was weird.

She widened her smile and pushed her chin up a notch. "I was thinking about the time machine in the movie. Going back, you know. Back to our past and, well, perhaps changing things."

Okay, that was really weird.

"Not that I'd want anything changed in my life, of course," Mom insisted and pushed a little harder on her smile. "I've had a magnificent life. So many wonderful things. You children . . ."

She'd mentioned me and my brother and sister first?

"And this beautiful home. Your father. Certainly your father. I've been blessed with so very many . . ."

Mom blinked quickly and gulped hard. She sipped her wine.

What the heck was going on? She was upset, something way beyond my-mascara-wand-is-clogged upset. Was she on the verge of tears?

I was totally at a loss. I'd never seen her like this before.

Even though we were at opposite ends of the personality scale, I had to hand it to Mom—at her core, she had grit.

She'd been hardened by years on the pageant circuit. She'd endured hours of spray tanning, two-sided tape, and over-the-counter meds used for purposes the manufacturer never intended. She'd learned to control her emotions—surely even Mom had eventually grown weary of the what-kind-of-vegetable-would-you-be type questions—and had learned early on to hold a smile and clap enthusiastically while another contestant took the crown she knew should have been hers.

"Mom? Mom, are you crying?" I walked closer.

"No. No, of course not." She turned her back to me and sniffed.

"Yes, you are," I insisted.

Okay, now I felt like a total idiot and horrible daughter. But Mom was always so pulled together—in her own way, of course. What was I supposed to do?

My first thought was to call someone to take over—which was bad of me, I know. But I'm not good at this sort of thing.

Was my sister home? She was great in situations like this. And what about my dad? Could I call him to come home from work and jump in here? He'd married her. He was legally obligated, right?

Yes, I could do those things, but Mom sniffed again and I knew this was all on me.

And I knew I could handle it.

"Mom?" I stepped in front of her. Tears pooled in her eyes. "Mom, tell me what's wrong."

She met my gaze and, I suppose, she was deciding for herself whether I could handle it.

"Tell me," I said.

She blinked back her tears and said, "Rumors have surfaced. Accusations have been made."

My thoughts scattered. Had Dad accused her of cheating? Had someone told Mom he had cheated on her?

"I heard something from one of my friends," Mom said. "You know, my standing luncheon with other pageant women."

Mom and a group of former pageant queens—whom I mentally referred to as a coven—met regularly to support ongoing beauty pageants, coach contestants, and give out advice.

Knowing the rumor came from one of them, my thoughts flew in a different direction.

Had somebody accused Mom of dyeing her hair with boxed color at home? Had they suggested she'd had work done?

"You recall that I was in the Miss California Cupid pageant?" Mom asked.

She'd been in dozens of pageants back before she'd met my dad. I didn't know one from the other.

"Sure," I said.

This was easier.

"It was my first truly important pageant. I was only nineteen," Mom said. "I took second place, but it got me noticed."

Oh, yeah. Now I remembered. It was early in her pageant career so, even though she'd come in second, she'd been thrilled.

"With that attention, I was able to get the recognition and, well, the confidence I needed to keep entering pageants," Mom said. "The Miss California Cupid contest was my stepping stone to national competitions."

Back before she'd married my dad and hung up her crown, Mom had been Miss California and third runner-up in the Miss America pageant.

"What kind of rumors and accusations are circulating?" I asked.

"It seems that someone with inside knowledge of the Miss California Cupid pageant during the year I competed is threatening to go public with allegations of wrongdoing," Mom said. "A conflict of interest involving a contestant and one of the judges."

That was it? A conflict of interest? That's what had Mom in tears?

I didn't get it.

"This could ruin everything," Mom said, and gulped down the last of her wine. "If a formal complaint is filed, the board of directors will have to take action. Crowns and titles will be stripped. The media, of course, will get involved."

Okay, I could imagine what bloggers and late-night talk show hosts would do with the situation.

"Who's making this claim?" I asked.

"I have no idea."

"Who's the judge?"

She waved my question away and said, "If this comes to light, everyone will be making tawdry remarks—forever. This will never be lived down or forgotten."

Mom didn't want the pageant that meant the most to her smeared by scandal. Even though I wasn't exactly on board with the whole beauty pageant thing, I couldn't stand by and do nothing to help.

"I'll check into it," I told her.

"You'll—you'll what?"

"I'll ask around," I said.

"No."

"I can find out who's involved."

Mom shook her head. "No. No, you mustn't."

She didn't know I'd been involved with a number of murder investigations and worked with a homicide detective and a private investigator.

"I can do this," I told her. "I know people who can help."

"I forbid it," she said, switching to her mom voice.

"But, Mom—"

She snapped into her pageant stance and said, "I refuse to be involved in this distasteful affair in any fashion. Certainly, no more attention should be drawn to it by pursuing the matter."

She had a point. The whole thing might lose steam and disappear if nobody was giving it any energy.

"Well, if you're sure," I said.

"I'm very sure." Mom looked relieved. "The less said, the better. And, please, don't mention this to anyone."

Since I didn't travel in pageant circles, I knew no one who'd want to know—or would have the least bit of interest in—this particular rumor.

"No problem," I said.

On my way out, I stopped by the kitchen and assured Juanita nothing serious was going on with Mom, then got in my Honda and headed for the closest Starbucks. Yes, I'd just had a Frappie on the drive over but, really, can you have too much chocolate and caffeine?

As I sat in the drive-through digging in my purse for my wallet, I pulled out the Holt's employee benefits handbook I'd grabbed from the assistant store managers' office earlier. The line stretched eight cars deep so I had some time to kill. I flipped to the chapter that detailed the Employee of the Month info.

Wow, this was a long chapter.

Under normal circumstances, being Employee of the Anything wasn't something I would aspire to. But it was a small price to pay to keep my discount at Nuovo.

The stunning Mystique clutch bag bloomed in my head. Yes, definitely worth it and, really, how hard could it be?

The line moved forward. I inched up a bit.

I skimmed the list of requirements and—oh my God. *Oh my God.*

Total panic mode swept over me.

To get the Employee of the Month award I'd have to develop a minimum of twenty credit card applications and ring up over five grand in sales. I'd have to sell two hundred dollars' worth of gift cards. That meant I'd have to work the checkout line and talk to the customers—actually provide service.

Plus, I couldn't be late for my shift one single time, and I would have to get a recommendation from the Rita, the cashiers' supervisor.

Oh, crap.

A car honked behind me. I pulled forward.

Jeez, employees at Holt's accomplished all of this?

I ordered my Frappie and slumped down in my seat.

How would I pull this off? Yeah, okay, I could do those things for a day—maybe—but for several weeks? And, surely, I wasn't the only person who'd thought of this. Everyone in the store would be vying for the award to ensure a transfer to another store—which meant I'd have to up my game considerably and do even more actual work.

I drove up to the window, paid, and grabbed my Frappuccino. Gulping it down, I pulled away, forcing my brain to think harder. There had to be a way to get around this. There had to be.

Then it hit me.

If Detectives Shuman and Madison solved

Asha's murder before the story gained any traction, the corporate office would have to scrap their plan to close the store.

Then something else hit me.

I didn't have to wait for Shuman and Madison. *I* could solve Asha's murder.

I hopped up and down and did a little dance in my seat as I drove away.

Oh my God, this was a brilliant idea—and it would be a heck of a lot easier than earning the Employee of the Month award.

Chapter 6

"I'm so very sorry, Ms. Randolph, but your Mystique bags haven't yet arrived."

I was on my cell phone with Chandra, my too-perfect-to-be-human personal shopper at Nuovo, as I inched toward the time clock along with the other Holt's employees reporting for our morning shift. My day already needed a boost. This news didn't help.

"No phones on the sales floor," Rita squawked from her if-only-this-position-came-with-a-gun stance by the whiteboard.

"Can you give me a firm date when they will arrive?" I asked.

"That means you, Princess."

"Your request is at the very top of our list," Chandra said. "Please rest assured we're giving this situation our utmost attention. You'll be the first person notified of the arrival of the shipment, Ms. Randolph."

She'd said it so nicely, all I could do was thank her.

I hate it when that happens.

From the corner of my eye I saw Rita mad-dogging me, so I kept the phone to my ear pretending I was talking, and glared right back until I punched in—which was kind of bad of me, I know, but it sure as heck gave my morning a boost.

With Rita still glaring, I went to my locker and pretended to put my cell phone into my handbag, but really slid it into the pocket of my jeans—no way could I be without my phone for my entire shift—and left the breakroom.

I'd hoped Nuovo would tell me my Mystique bags were ready for pickup soon. Losing my employee discount if Holt's closed before the bags arrived was a real concern—as any true shopper would know. Of course, I didn't intend to just stand around and hope for the best, when finding Asha's murderer would solve the problem.

I hadn't heard from Detective Shuman with any more information about the investigation. I didn't have to stand around and hope for the best from him, either. I knew where I could find what I needed to get started.

Instead of heading onto the sales floor, I went to the assistant store managers' office. Nobody was inside, as usual—jeez, maybe I should apply for the position since, apparently, you never had to be in there doing any work. The file cabinet beside the desk was unlocked so I went through the drawers until I found Asha's personnel file.

I didn't want to hang around in case somebody wandered in, so I pulled out my cell phone and snapped pictures of Asha's employment application, her résumé, and the new hire documents she'd completed during orientation.

I knew she hadn't worked at Holt's for long, so I checked the dates. She'd been hired just before Thanksgiving, in time for the Christmas shopping rush, and had left in mid-December; no reason for her departure was given. She'd only lasted about three weeks—not that I blamed her, of course.

Still, I wondered why Asha hadn't been here for the entire Christmas season. Holt's was desperate for sales clerks at that time of year so I figured she must have done something horrendous to get fired. Sandy had mentioned she'd quit for a better-paying job. Maybe that's all there was to it.

I slid Asha's personnel folder back into the cabinet, closed the drawer, and headed for the—well, heck, I'd forgotten to check the schedule by the time clock and see where I was supposed to work this morning. I slipped into the breakroom. Bella was there, standing in front of the vending machine.

She pointed to the whiteboard, where her name was written, and said, "I was two minutes late—two minutes—and Rita wrote me up."

"I hate her."

"Damn straight." Bella ripped open the bag of chips she'd just gotten from the vending machine and sat down at a table. "So I decided, since I already got written up I may as well enjoy it."

"Makes sense," I told her.

In fact, it made a lot of sense. I sat down across from her.

"Have you heard anything else about the store closing?" Bella asked.

"I talked to Jeanette. It could definitely happen," I said. "I can't stop wondering why Asha was out back by the loading dock."

"Beats me," Bella said, munching on her chips.

"Do you remember seeing her in the store after she quit?" I asked.

I didn't recall ever seeing her, but it was my personal customer service policy to avoid eye contact with anyone I encountered on the sales floor, so even if she'd been here I might have missed her.

"She probably came back to shop for something," Bella said and shrugged. "Most everybody comes back, sooner or later. The stuff here is pretty cheap, and Asha didn't seem like she was exactly raking in the cash."

"I'll ask around," I said.

Bella paused, a chip halfway to her lips. "You're sticking your nose into this because of that hot PI, aren't you? What's his name? Jack. Yeah, him."

The mention of Jack's name sent a wave of—of—well, something through me. I didn't know how I'd face him when I still couldn't recall exactly what had happened the other night. Thank God I hadn't heard from him.

"Jack isn't involved in Asha's murder investigation," I told Bella.

"Get him involved," Bella insisted. "He's one fine-looking man. He needs to come into the store, make my day better."

"If you come up with any information about Asha, maybe he will," I said.

"Hot damn. I'm on the case."

Bella rushed out of the breakroom. I erased her name from the whiteboard and followed her out.

It was a Louis Vuitton afternoon. Definitely a Louis Vuitton afternoon.

When my shift ended at Holt's, I swung by my apartment and morphed into Event Planner Extraordinaire—my idea of a superhero in designer fashions—by changing into one of my fabulous Chanel business suits, and headed for L.A. Affairs. Business was slow this month—especially for me, since I'd refused to plan any romantic Valentine's Day celebrations for anyone who wasn't me—so the planners took turns reporting to the office to handle any new clients who might come in and, of course, check on our upcoming events.

The L.A. Affairs office was located at the intersection of Sepulveda and Ventura in Sherman Oaks, one of L.A.'s many upscale areas. Everyone dressed in fabulous clothes and carried equally fabulous handbags to impress our well-to-do clientele—which I was totally on board with.

I pulled into the parking garage, took the elevator up to the third floor, and walked into the office. Mindy, our receptionist, was at her desk. She was fortyish, round in places that should have been flat, and had blond hair that, for some reason, she'd recently permed.

She looked like a tumbleweed had crash landed on her head.

"Are you ready to party?" she chanted.

That ridiculous slogan was meant for clients but, for some reason, I was continually subjected to it.

"I work here," I told her for what seemed like whatever-comes-after-a-trillion times.

"Oh, yes. You're Haley, aren't you?" Mindy said, nodding. "Yes, that's who you are. Haley."

"Yes, I'm Haley. I work here. So you don't have to keep repeating that slogan every time you see me."

"Oh. Okay. I understand," Mindy said. "Got it."

"Good," I said, and walked away.

"Have a nice afternoon, Hannah," Mindy called.

Good grief.

One of the many awesome things about L.A. Affairs was that I had my own private office. It was done in neutrals with splashes of blue and yellow, and had a huge window that overlooked the Galleria, a great shopping center, across the street. I stowed my handbag in the bottom drawer of my desk and, of course, headed for the breakroom.

I helped myself to coffee from the big pot

that was always brewing, and finished it off with a generous splash of French vanilla creamer and too-numerous-to-count packets of sugar. Just as I was eyeing the box of doughnuts on the counter and deciding between chocolate-covered and chocolate-covered-with-sprinkles—really, it was a big decision—my L.A. Affairs BFF walked in.

Kayla was about my age, with dark hair and lots of curves. She had on a black Michael Kors suit, and totally rocked it.

"Thank God you're here," Kayla said, helping herself to coffee. "This place has been like a morgue all week."

"No way," I said. "What have I missed?"

"Nothing."

"No, really. What's going on?"

"Nothing. Really."

Okay, that was weird.

"There must be something," I said. "Rumors, gossip?"

"None of that," she said.

Oh my God, did that mean *I* was the one spreading all the rumors and gossip?

Apparently so.

Well, somebody had to do it.

I grabbed two doughnuts, a chocolate-covered and a chocolate-covered-with-sprinkles—no sense wearing myself out with decisions so early in the afternoon—and left the breakroom.

I settled into my desk ready to buckle down and get things handled. I hadn't been in the office for a while, so I had a lot to catch up on.

I started with Facebook, of course.

Sipping my coffee, I ate my doughnuts as I updated my page, then checked my bank balance, read my horoscope, and booked a pedi. I took a selfie sitting at my desk and sent it to Marcie, asking if she wanted to go shopping tonight, then pulled up the Macy's website to look for jeans when my desk phone rang.

"Hello? Hello, is Hannah there?"

Oh, crap.

It was Mindy.

"This is Haley," I told her.

"Is Hannah there?" she asked.

"No, Mindy," I said—and I sounded really nice about it, sort of. "There is no Hannah. It's me. Haley."

"When will Hannah be back?" she asked. "I have a message for her."

"Listen carefully. There is no—never mind. I'll give her the message," I said.

Really, there's only so much I can take.

"Tell her there's a man here to see her. He's in interview room three—four. Four. Yes, four. Or maybe it's three." Mindy giggled and said, "And, oh goodness, is he a handsome thing. Very handsome."

My thoughts scattered as I slammed down the phone.

A handsome—a very handsome—man was here to see me? Mentally, I ran through the upcoming events I was planning for clients—a couple of St. Patrick's Day parties, some birthdays, an anniversary—but none of them involved a man, let alone a handsome one.

Then it hit me. Oh my God, it must be Jack Bishop. What was I going to tell him? How was I supposed to act? I still didn't have a clue exactly what had gone on at his place.

I drew in a breath to calm myself—it didn't help—and left my office. I was going to play it cool, somehow, no matter what.

I stepped into interview room four and there stood Liam Douglas. Yikes! I hadn't even considered that Liam was here to see me.

Am I a crappy sort-of girlfriend, or what?

He smiled—Liam had a killer smile. He was tall, sturdy, with long limbs and a good build. His hair was light brown—blond in certain light—and he had brilliant green eyes. Today he had on a Tom Ford suit that fit perfectly.

Since he was an attorney for the law firm that represented L.A. Affairs and we'd decided not to broadcast our relationship, we remained a respectable distance apart.

"I hope you don't mind my dropping by," he said. "I knew you were coming in this afternoon."

Liam was the kind of guy who asked questions and actually remembered the answers—I know because I'd quizzed him.

"It's great to see you," I said and, really, it was.

"I wanted to talk to you about—sorry." Liam pulled his cell phone from the inside pocket of his jacket, read the screen, then shook his head.

"I wasn't expecting this to come up today. I have to go. Sorry."

He'd been super understanding about the long hours I'd put in over the Christmas party season, my last-minute cancellations, and the interruptions during the few occasions we'd tried to squeeze in some time together so, really, I was okay with it.

"Sure, no problem," I said.

But he didn't leave right away. He gazed at me for a moment—I mean, really, gazed at me—and said, "Will you have dinner with me?"

This didn't seem like the usual let's-get-together invitation I'd been getting from him.

"Soon?" he added.

Something else was definitely going on.

"If you're planning to stop seeing me, you'd better tell me now," I said. "I'm not above making a big scene in public."

Liam smiled as if he thought that was the cutest thing he'd ever heard, and said, "No, Haley, never seeing you again is the very last thing I want."

Some crazy heat jumped from him to me, and I couldn't help smiling.

"Okay, dinner," I said.

"Soon."

"Soon," I agreed.

"Perfect." He gave me one last killer smile, and left the interview room.

Some of the warmth seemed to go with him. Weird, huh?

I headed back to my office, suddenly restless.

One of the things I liked best about working

at L.A. Affairs was that the management didn't expect me to sit at my desk all day. In fact, they preferred I was out meeting with clients, inspecting venues, and interviewing new vendors.

Since, luckily, none of my scheduled events needed much attention at the moment, I grabbed my handbag from my desk drawer and left.

Chapter 7

When I got into my Honda in the parking garage, my cell phone chimed. It was a text message from Marcie. She was all-in for shopping tonight, as a BFF would be. Of course, I didn't really need any of the jeans I'd looked at online earlier—and I doubted Marcie did, either—but that was no reason not to check them out.

I texted her back suggesting we meet at the mall in Sherman Oaks, since I was already here, and just as I was about to drop my cell phone into my handbag, it chirped again.

A message from Liam appeared, asking if dinner tonight was too soon. I couldn't help smiling. We'd been taking things slowly—I'm not one to jump into a relationship too fast and, as it turned out, neither is he—and I was starting to feel a warm glow inside when I thought about him.

Still, no matter how much I was glowing internally, I couldn't accept the dinner invitation. I'd already committed to shopping with Marcie.

Yeah, okay, I could have blown off our plans and she would have understood, but I wasn't going to cancel with a friend because a sort-of boyfriend had asked me out. That's how I roll. And it had nothing to do with Macy's winter clearance sale on jeans. I swear.

I texted Liam back, explaining that I already had plans and I couldn't make dinner. His reply came a couple of minutes later in the form of a sad emoji, but no suggestion for a future dinner date.

Huh. What did that mean? Had he changed his mind about wanting to see me *soon*? Had I offended him?

Good grief. Boyfriends—even sort-of boyfriends—were a lot of trouble.

I'd have to talk to Marcie about it tonight.

To distract myself, I sat in my car for a few minutes mentally accessorizing the new jeans I would likely buy tonight, and the Mystique clutch popped into my head—I don't know why; that sort of thing just happened from time to time.

No way could I carry the Mystique with jeans. That meant, of course, I would need a new dress.

Then the whole picture shattered with the unwelcome thought that I wouldn't get the Mystique at a huge discount if the Holt's store closed and I lost my job. Asha's murder investigation bloomed in my head.

I pulled out my cell phone and found the pics I'd snapped of the documents in her employment file. Her résumé indicated she'd had a long series of jobs over the past eighteen months or so, mostly for small companies, probably for minimum wage, which explained why she drove that crappy old car. She'd lasted no more than a few weeks at each place.

What the heck was up with her? Why was she job hopping? Was it her, or was it the employers?

I figured there could be any number of reasons for so many changes. Maybe she had a health issue that caused her to call out so often she'd been let go. Maybe she was hiding something like a drug or alcohol problem. There was always the possibility that she simply got bored at the jobs—I could totally relate—or just hadn't found her niche yet. Or maybe nobody could stand to work with her because she was a raging bitch.

One of the places Asha had worked caught my eye. Cakes By Carrie was a bakery in the Holt's shopping center. She'd worked there a couple of months before she'd taken the sales clerk job at Holt's.

Maybe that explained one of the questions I'd had about Asha's death.

Her body was found near the loading dock. I'd wondered why she'd been at the rear of the Holt's store in the first place. She must have gone to the bakery to visit a friend and they'd stepped out back to chat or maybe have a smoke. Somehow, that had led to Asha's murder.

I was definitely going to have to see what was up at Cakes By Carrie.

I scrolled to the employment application Asha had filled out at Holt's. It indicated she lived in an apartment complex here in Sherman Oaks. I punched the address into my GPS. It was less than a mile away.

Since I was so close—and L.A. Affairs was paying me—I decided this was a great time to check it out.

I wound down the ramps in the parking garage and turned right on Sepulveda, drove a few blocks, then nearly rear-ended the car in front of me when I saw the place. Oh my God, it was gorgeous.

I whipped into their parking lot and nosed into a space.

The complex was small, immaculate, very upscale and elegant.

Jeez, Asha had lived here? No way.

I double-checked the address. Yep, this was Asha's apartment building.

I accessed their website. In the photos, the units looked exceptional. The list of amenities included custom walnut hardwood floors, imported tile, stainless-steel appliances, granite countertops with mosaic glass backsplashes, and hand-distressed custom cabinetry. There was wainscoting, designer paint, and huge walk-in closets with custom shelving, as well as upgraded fixtures and hardware, and decorative doors and baseboards. There was a landscaped pool and spa area, a game room, a gym, and a rooftop lounge. A two-bedroom rented for three grand per month.

Three grand? How the heck did Asha afford a place like this?

Unless she was a trust-fund baby with mental issues—which was entirely possible—Asha must have had a generous, altruistic roommate, or maybe a live-in boyfriend with a great job.

I had to find out what was going on. I considered going inside and talking to the resident manager, but no way would anyone who worked here reveal any info about their renters. I'd have to check out the place myself.

If two renters were on the lease, which was a definite possibility, the apartment would have been assigned two parking spaces. I decided to see if, by chance, Asha's roommate's car was there. If so, I'd just go up and knock on the door. I was, technically, a sort-of friend of Asha's come to pay respects.

A wrought-iron gate covered the entrance to the underground parking, so I waited until another car went through, then followed it inside. The place was full of expensive cars—Mercedes, BMW, Cadillac—and I could only imagine how the owners had turned up their noses at the sight of Asha's way-past-its-prime Chevy parked nearby.

The parking spaces were numbered so I cruised around until I came to the two that were assigned to Asha's apartment.

I slammed on the brakes.

What the heck?

One of the spaces was empty. In the other sat Asha's banged-up Chevy.

How could that be? Detective Shuman told me they'd towed it from the Holt's parking lot and handed it over to the lab guys as part of the murder investigation.

I hopped out of my car and peered in the Chevy's windows—careful not to touch anything, of course. I spotted a couple of empty water bottles, a crumbled bag from Taco Bell, and a pair of flip-flops—no note from the murderer confessing to Asha's death, unfortunately.

I snapped a pic of the license plate and got back in my car.

None of this made any sense. I needed to talk to Detective Shuman—plus, my brain definitely needed a boost.

First things first.

I headed for Starbucks.

Shuman stood beside a table at Starbucks's outdoor seating area at the Galleria when I walked up. I'd called him before I left Asha's apartment complex, asking if he could meet me. I'd also sent the photo of the license plate and requested that he check with the DMV.

He was on his cell phone, grinning. I knew what that meant.

On the table sat a black coffee and a mocha Frappuccino. Shuman knew my favorite drink, and he'd obviously picked up on my distress when I'd called him because he'd ordered me a *venti*.

Shuman caught sight of me, turned away and whispered something into the phone, then tucked it into his jacket pocket.

"You'd be terrible undercover," I told him. "I know that was Brittany you were talking to."

His grin widened, giving me my answer.

"How's it going with you two?" I asked as we sat down.

Shuman sipped his coffee. "Good."

He'd been dating Brittany for a few months. She was nineteen, tall, blond, and overflowing with energy. She was Shuman's transition girlfriend; he'd lost his long-time serious love interest not long before meeting her. I figured their relationship would have run its course by now, but not so. Shuman seemed happy. That's all that mattered.

"What about you?" he asked.

I sipped my Frappie and said, "He's still off somewhere finding himself."

Shuman gave me a funny look and said, "I thought you were dating that lawyer. Liam."

Oh, crap.

My mind had automatically jumped to Ty. What was wrong with me?

"Well, Liam and I are sort of dating," I said, hoping I didn't sound like as big of an idiot as I felt.

This seemed like a great time to change the subject.

"Please tell me you've figured out what was up with Asha," I said. "Because everything I'm finding makes no sense."

"Such as?"

I could see that Shuman was in semi-cop-mode and reluctant to dole out info, which didn't suit me, but I had no choice but to roll with it.

"You told me you'd had her car towed from the Holt's parking lot," I said.

"We did."

"I just saw it at her apartment complex." I wiggled my finger at the pocket of his jacket where he kept his cell phone. "That's the license plate I sent you. Did you run it?"

He nodded. "It's a Chevrolet, and it's registered to Asha."

"How could it be at her apartment if you towed it away?"

"We towed a BMW," Shuman said.

Okay, I was surprised.

"Both cars are currently registered to Asha," he told me.

I figured Shuman hadn't bothered to take the Chevrolet to the lab since it wasn't at the crime scene. But I knew he'd been inside her apartment.

"How did her place look?" I asked.

"A hell of a lot nicer than mine, that's for sure," Shuman said. "We took a number of items into evidence. The lab is working on them."

"Did Asha have a roommate, or something?" I asked.

"According to the apartment manager, Asha's name was the only one on the lease."

Now I was shocked.

"How did she afford it on minimum wage?" I asked.

"Bank records indicate she had just shy of fifty thousand in her account."

"Oh my God, you're kidding."

Shuman gave me an I-don't-get-it-either shrug and said, "Could have been that she was into something illegal. Maybe her dad was supporting her, or a sugar daddy."

We both lapsed into silence while he sipped his coffee and I drained half of my Frappie. Either of those scenarios could have been correct—or something entirely different might have been going on with Asha.

"No, it's more than that," I said. "Asha drove that old junker to work every day. She wanted everybody to see her in it and think she didn't have much money. Why would she do that?"

"We'll find out eventually. We're still looking at surveillance video at the shopping center, canvassing the stores, looking for witnesses." Shuman stood. "I have to go. Let me know if you find out anything else."

"Sure," I said.

But, really, I wasn't paying much attention to Shuman as he walked away. The image of Asha kept circling through my brain.

Obviously, she had been leading a double life. But why?

CHAPTER 8

"Haley?"

I turned at the mention of my name and nearly reeled back in horror. In the breakroom doorway stood Jeanette, wearing a pantsuit covered in huge green, red, yellow, and white florals.

She looked like Hawaii.

The entire state.

"Come by my office before you go to the sales floor," Jeanette said, and walked away.

The employees ahead of me in line for the time clock all turned and glared.

"What did you do this time?" one of the girls asked. "Get us all pay reductions?"

"Causing the store to close wasn't enough for you?" a guy asked. "What now? Our medical is getting cancelled?"

"This isn't my fault," I said.

Well, okay, it kind of was. But I was confident there was a way to blame someone else.

Before I could come up with anything, the line moved forward, everybody grumbling as they clocked in. I hung back a little, then punched in my employee code and pressed my thumb to the scanner, marking the beginning of another four hours I'd never get back and, hopefully, wouldn't remember.

According to the schedule hanging above the time clock, I was supposed to work in the housewares department today. On my own personal scale of crappy places to be, this department was ranked near the bottom because it offered one major benefit. You could keep a customer waiting a really long time while in the stockroom pretending you were wrestling those huge boxes of pots and pans off the shelves when you were actually texting friends, and nobody would be the wiser.

But first I had to see Jeanette. I went to her office door, braced myself, and walked inside.

Her outfit didn't seem so hideous this time—which was alarming on a certain level—because she was seated behind her desk. She gestured to a chair and I sat down.

"Good news," Jeanette declared. "The store has been granted something of a reprieve."

She looked positively grim, so I wondered how good this news really was. Still, my heart beat a little faster thinking the store would remain open long enough for me to get my Mystique clutch.

That may sound selfish but, really, I was just being practical.

"Our corporate office has arranged for a team of investigative journalists from a major television network to come to the store," she said. "They are doing an extensive exposé on us."

I didn't know why Jeanette was telling me this, unless maybe she really hadn't heard that Ty and I had broken up.

I saw no reason to point it out.

"It's felt that if the report goes well, our public image will be restored and closure won't be necessary," Jeanette said.

Then something else hit me and my heart beat a lot faster—but for a different reason.

Oh my God, corporate had done this? Did that mean Ty was back? Was he in his office now, calling the shots?

Jeanette kept talking, but it turned into blah-blah-blah. All I could focus on was Ty. Had he really returned? Was he back and hadn't called me? Had his months of solitude and soul searching caused him to realize he never wanted to see me again? Or was he planning to surprise me with a fantastic I'm-back confession of how he couldn't live without me, how miserable he'd been while he was away, how he'd longed for me every second of every day until—

"What do you think, Haley?" Jeanette asked.

Oh, crap.

At moments like this—which happened way too often, probably—I'd learned that if I kept quiet and looked thoughtful long enough, the other person would eventually say something that would give me some clue as to what the conversation had been about and just what kind of response I was expected to make.

Jeanette didn't let me down.

"You know these two detectives. Do you think they can solve this case quickly?" she asked.

Okay. I had this.

"I spoke with Detective Shuman yesterday," I said.

Jeanette looked surprised and impressed.

I hurried on before she could ask for details and said, "Progress has already been made in the case. Asha's death is their top priority."

"It's imperative this investigation is concluded, the murder is solved, and everything is wrapped up before the journalists arrive," Jeanette said. "This is a golden opportunity to save the store. We won't get another chance like this."

I decided this was a good time to try and get more information for my own investigation.

"Did you know Asha well?" I asked.

"I make it a point to know all my employees," she told me.

I knew that was standard company b.s., but didn't say so.

"Did it seem odd to you that Asha quit after working here for only a few weeks?" I asked.

"Some employees leave quickly." Her expression soured a bit. "And others I can't get rid of quickly enough."

She wasn't talking about me, was she?

Well, no sense in dwelling on that aspect of the conversation. I had a murder to solve.

I left Jeanette's office feeling pretty darn good about the possibility that the store might remain open. Really, the investigative journalists' report could be a blessing—or could blow up in corporate's face—but at least something was in the works and there was a chance it would succeed.

As I made my way through the store to my assigned section of purgatory in housewares, my cell phone vibrated in my pocket. I slipped into the lingerie department, ducked down between two racks of bras, and checked its ID screen. Marcie had sent me a text.

She'd cancelled our shopping trip last night, which I had been okay with. She'd told me why, but, since I'd been kind of wrapped up in my own problems, I hadn't been listening—which was bad of me, I know. If Marcie had noticed, she hadn't said anything, a typical best-friend move.

In her text she asked if we could try again tonight. I texted back to count me there.

Since I was already in this secluded spot in lingerie and nobody was around—and because my morning could always use a boost—I called Nuovo.

Chandra answered. I identified myself and she immediately launched into an apology.

"I'm so very sorry for the inconvenience, Ms. Randolph," she said. "Our shipment of Mystique bags hasn't arrived yet. We expect it any day now."

I was pretty sure that's what she'd told me the last time I called.

"What's the delay?" I asked.

"No delay," Chandra insisted. "Simply time in transit. Nothing unusual. Nothing at all."

I wasn't sure I really believed her, but I didn't want to put any bad mojo out into the world, so I thanked her and hung up.

Not exactly the boost I was looking for.

Crap.

I headed for housewares.

I clocked out exactly two seconds after my shift ended, grabbed my handbag—an adorable Coach tote—and left the store.

All I'd been able to think about during the last four hours of mindless shelf-stocking was Asha's murder—with thoughts of the Mystique woven through occasionally—and now I was anxious to get on with my investigation. I figured the easiest—and probably the tastiest—place to start was the bakery.

According to Asha's employment application and résumé, she'd worked at Cakes By Carrie for a few weeks before she'd taken the sales clerk position at Holt's. I'd theorized that Asha had gone back to visit, and that she and a friend had stepped out so they could talk. I hoped that my idea was right and that whoever her friend was had seen something helpful.

Shuman had mentioned he and Madison were still canvassing the area, looking for witnesses. I didn't know if they'd gotten to the bakery yet or, if they had, whether or not Shuman would tell me everything he'd uncovered. Yes, we were friends and exchanged info, but Shuman was still a cop and he had to be careful about leaking facts in an ongoing investigation.

I headed down the sidewalk toward the line of stores that spread out next to Holt's. The parking lot was crowded. Lots of people were out.

While Holt's anchored the center—it was by far the largest and the one that drew most of the shoppers—the other stores did a brisk business. They were mostly specialty shops—a craft store, a cigar shop, a convenience store, one of those mail and shipping centers. There was a furniture store that I was convinced was a drug front—but maybe I'd binged on *Breaking Bad* too many times—and, of course, the bakery.

The delicious smell of something sweet led me down the sidewalk, and just as I got to the bakery entrance, my cell phone rang. I checked the ID screen. Mom was calling. Against my better judgment, I answered.

"Hi, sweetie. How are you?" she asked.

She wanted to know how I was doing? Okay, that was weird.

"Are you all right, Mom?"

"Yes, of course. I'm fine. Perfectly fine. Absolutely nothing is wrong," she said. "Would you mind running by my travel agent's office and picking up something for me, honey? I would really appreciate it. If you have time, of course."

Mom had been friends with her travel agent since before she'd married my dad, and she always enjoyed catching up on news when a vacation was in the works, so this was hardly the kind of thing she'd ever asked me to do before.

"You're sure you're feeling okay, Mom?"

"Certainly," she told me. "Of course I'm fine."

I wasn't all that excited about going to the travel agent and listening to back-in-the-day stories about the two of them, but what could I do? Mom was Mom.

"Sure," I said. "I'll bring them to you later today."

"Thank you, honey," she said and we ended the call.

Now I desperately needed something from the bakery—and it had to be chocolate.

A little bell chimed when I walked inside. The place smelled great. It was decorated in pink and aqua, with splashes of white and just a touch of pale yellow. Several small tables and chairs with pink checked seats were arranged near the windows.

The display cases and shelves gleamed and were filled with fanciful cupcakes, cakes, cookies, and jars of candy. A six-tier wedding cake, an extravagant kid's birthday cake, and a lavish Valentine's Day cake were featured in niches around the room.

The girl behind the counter had on an aqua apron with "Cakes By Carrie" written in white. I figured her for maybe a few years older than me. Her blond hair was tied up with a pink scarf, and her waistline looked as if she'd sampled every treat the bakery had ever produced.

I waited until she finished with the mom and little girl at the counter, then stepped up when they left.

"Hi, I'm Haley," I said and smiled. "I work at Holt's."

She gave me a huge smile in return and said, "I'm Carrie."

I was a little surprised, since she seemed kind of young to own a bakery. But the place looked and smelled great, and it had been open for a while now so I figured she must know what she was doing.

"What can I get for you?" Carrie asked.

I gestured around the room and said, "I'd like the left side of the shop, please."

Her smile widened and she said, "Would you like that to go, or will you be enjoying it here?"

We both laughed.

"Just give me a half dozen of the every cupcake that has chocolate in it, please," I said.

Carrie fetched a pink bakery box and started filling it.

Even though my brain was overloaded with thoughts of massive amounts of sugar and chocolate, I forced myself to get on with the reason I'd come here.

I can push through when I have to.

"I guess you were pretty upset about what happened at Holt's the other day—you know, the murder," I said. "Asha was a friend of yours, wasn't she?"

Carrie froze. A few seconds ticked by as she stood as still as a cake topper. Then her eyes widened and she screamed, "*Asha* died? Asha *McLean*? It was *her?*"

I went into semi-panic mode—Carrie was in total-panic mode.

"Oh my God. I thought you knew," I told her. See how bad I am at this sort of thing?

"Oh, no . . . oh, no," Carrie wailed.

She dropped the bakery box and wobbled back and forth. I thought she was going to faint. I dashed around the display counter and put my arm around her shoulders.

"Jeez, I'm sorry," I said. "I didn't know you hadn't heard the news. I wouldn't have just blurted it out like that, if I'd known."

"Oh no . . ." she moaned.

"Come sit down."

I guided her across the shop and eased her into one of the chairs near the display window.

"Keep breathing," I said, then dashed behind the counter again, got a cup of water from the soda machine, and brought it back. "Here, drink this."

I dropped into the chair next to her and waited while she sipped the water and caught her breath. Finally, some of the color came back into her cheeks.

"I'm so sorry. Really," I said.

"It's okay," she said. "I guess I should have known about it already. But I don't have time for the gossip that circulates through the shopping center. I have too much to do. I can't spare the time."

"I know Asha used to work here," I said. "I guess you two stayed friends after she left, huh?"

More color flooded Carrie's cheeks, and she downed the water.

"Yes, you could say that, I guess, sort of," she said.

"Did you see her that day? The day she, you know, died?" I asked.

Okay, maybe that seemed kind of heartless, but I had to find out if Carrie had been with Asha out back and had witnessed anything.

"I didn't even know she was here that day," Carrie said. She slumped into the chair and said, "I can't believe this. My goodness, what's going to happen now?"

"Don't worry," I said, glad I could give her some good news. "It looks like Holt's might not close after all, so—"

"Holt's is going to close?" She bolted upright in the chair. "It can't close!"

Oh my God. Not again.

"It's our anchor store! If it closes, my bakery will be ruined!"

"No, no, listen."

I waved my hands trying to calm her.

"All the stores will be ruined!"

Note to self—hand waving accomplishes nothing.

"Listen—you have to listen," I insisted.

I grabbed her hand and patted it—although I'm sure bitch-slapping her would have been more effective—until she calmed down a bit.

"Holt's isn't going to close," I told her. "Plans are in the works. Everything is going to be fine."

She gulped. "Are you sure?"

I was afraid to answer truthfully—can you blame me?

"You have a great shop here. It's going to be fine, no matter what happens," I said. "I know because I've been inside a lot of bakeries—a lot of them."

"It's terribly hard to keep a small business going," she said and tears pooled in her eyes.

Oh, no, not tears. I couldn't handle a crier right now.

"But yours is succeeding," I told her and patted her hand a little harder.

She plastered her palm against her forehead and shook her head. "You don't know what I've been through."

"I know it's tough," I said. "Your bakery is fantastic. Really. Customers love it."

I didn't know that for an actual fact but, come on, it was a bakery—who wouldn't love it?

Carrie was quiet for a minute or two, then withdrew her hand from mine and took in a deep breath.

"I shouldn't go borrowing trouble—that's what Mom always says," she said softly.

"Good advice," I said.

I gave it another minute—well, okay, about half that time—then hopped up and circled behind the display counter. I picked up the box of cupcakes she'd dropped which, luckily, had landed flat and nothing had spilled out.

"Are you going to be okay?" I asked.

"I think so," Carrie said. "And thank you, Haley, thank you for giving me the news. You did the right thing."

Her eyes were puffy. Her cheeks were red. Her cute little pink scarf was askew.

Oh yeah, I felt great about it.

I whipped a twenty from my wallet and stuck it next to the cash register, grabbed the box of cupcakes, and left.

Chapter 9

My interview with Carrie—okay, it wasn't much of an interview, but it sounds better than calling it the I-thought-I-was-giving-her-a-stroke talk that it really was—hadn't revealed anything substantial, as I'd hoped. All I'd gotten from her was that she hadn't even known Asha was at the shopping center that day. She hadn't been out back by the Dumpster. She hadn't witnessed anything.

Still, Carrie had gotten so upset upon hearing that Asha was dead, I figured they'd been pretty good friends. Maybe I could talk to her again, though, really, I wasn't looking forward to it.

I was on the 405 headed for Studio City, where Mom's travel agent had her office. After leaving Cakes By Carrie, I'd dashed into my apartment and changed out of my Holt's-appropriate jeans and sweater, and into yet another jeans and sweater outfit, this one costing considerably more.

I transitioned onto the 101, slightly bummed that the whole bakery thing had been a dead end. I wasn't any closer to uncovering who was behind Asha's death or what was up with the double life she had apparently been leading. I had to figure out my next move.

Jack Bishop popped into my head.

He was a private investigator so he had access to all sorts of databases that I didn't, plus he seemed to know absolutely everyone and everything about them. I could ask him to check into Asha's murder—except that I still didn't know how to act around him.

That whole thing made me feel yucky.

Then it occurred to me that Jack still hadn't called me, and I started to feel slightly miffed. What was that all about?

I mean, come on, I woke up at his place. Didn't good manners require a phone call from him?

Honestly, I didn't know. I'd never been in this situation before.

I definitely had to talk to Marcie about this during our shopping trip later today.

The Laurel Canyon exit came into view so I cut over two lanes, took the off-ramp, and turned into a shopping center near Ventura Boulevard. A wide variety of businesses occupied the complex, which was squeezed onto a lot that also included a restaurant, a yogurt shop, and a dance studio. The travel agency had a place on the ground floor. I parked and went inside.

The office was cluttered with travel posters, travel books, travel everything. The place was hopping. Several customers waited on comfy chairs, while others crowded around the desks of the agents who were helping them. The receptionist was on the phone, and two more lines were ringing.

I checked nameplates and spotted Courtney, Mom's friend, sitting in the back corner. She was about the same age as my mom, tall, slender, with dark hair, very attractive. The two of them had been in pageants together back in the day. Mom had told me all about it—I think. I'd drifted off.

Courtney looked up from her computer, past the couple sitting at her desk, and spotted me.

"Haley?" she called, smiling as if I, rather than my mom, were her old friend, which was kind of weird because I didn't recall ever meeting her. "You're Haley, aren't you? I knew it was you. Caroline said you were coming by. Come on back."

She waved me over to her desk and held out a thick envelope.

"She's going to love this," Courtney told me. "The itinerary is perfect. It's everything she asked for, and then some."

"Thanks," I said, and tucked the envelope into my tote.

Her smile widened. "And tell her to stop being such a stranger. We need to have that lunch."

"Thanks, again," I said, and left.

I'd told Marcie that I would meet her at The

Grove, so I hopped back on the freeway. Since I'd worked at Holt's this morning and I wasn't on L.A. Affair's schedule today, we were meeting somewhere closer for her. I made pretty good time, left my Honda in the parking garage, and took the elevator to the ground floor.

A wide variety of upscale stores, both large and small, was located here, along with restaurants and a movie theater. The storefronts ringed a pedestrian-only street where an old-fashioned trolley carried shoppers from the stores to the farmer's market located at the other end of the complex. A water fountain danced and swayed to all different types of music.

I checked my phone and read a text from Marcie telling me she was already here. I was about to call her when I spotted her standing outside Nordstrom.

"Ready to shop?" she asked, when I walked up.

I was always ready to shop.

"Okay if we hit the Coach store first?" I asked.

Marcie froze. "What's wrong?"

"Nothing."

She gave me her BFF look and said, "If you need to get a handbag fix first thing, something's wrong. Come on."

Is she a great friend or what?

We walked down the street to the first restaurant we came to and got a seat on the outdoor patio. It was almost dark now, so the twinkle lights were on and candles burned on the tables. Faint music played somewhere.

"Wine?" Marcie asked, when the waiter stopped at our table.

Yikes! No way was I drinking wine after what had happened the last time.

"Just a soda," I told him.

Marcie ordered the same, plus chips and salsa, and he left.

"Okay, what is it?" she asked.

Jeez, where to start?

I hadn't told Marcie about waking up at Jack's place. I'd intended to, but I couldn't bring myself to do it right now—maybe this was one of those things even a BFF shouldn't know.

I decided to tackle first the problem that put me in the best light—which is kind of bad, but there it was.

"Liam," I said. "When I saw him yesterday, he gave me one of *those* looks and asked if we could have dinner. *Soon.*"

"You're kidding." Marcie leaned forward. "Like maybe he wants to move your relationship further along?"

I nodded, then paused while the waiter served our food and drinks.

"But that's great," Marcie insisted. She stopped with a chip half dunked into the salsa. "Isn't it?"

"Well, yes," I said.

"You like him, don't you?"

"I do. He's smart, he's funny, he pays attention when I talk," I said. "He's always been there if I needed something, but he doesn't smother me. He was super understanding when I had to work so much over the holidays."

"He's totally hot," Marcie insisted, munching

on a chip. "So what's the problem—oh my God, Haley. It's Ty, isn't it?"

She'd said it like she was shocked and disappointed.

I couldn't blame her.

As a best friend would, she took a breath and calmed down.

"You're not over him," she said. "Still."

"What's wrong with me?" I asked.

Jeez, I knew I was being an idiot about the whole thing with Ty, but I couldn't seem to stop myself.

"There's something about Ty," I said, "that I can't let go of."

Marcie nodded thoughtfully and said, "Is he back from his sabbatical, or whatever it is, yet?"

"I haven't heard a word from him."

"Have you called him?" she asked.

I shook my head. "I figured he needed time and solitude to work out whatever is going on with him."

"But if you knew he was back but hadn't called you, that would pretty much end things with him, wouldn't it?" she asked.

"He wouldn't do something that crappy."

"Have you tried to find out if he's back—without contacting him directly?" Marcie asked. "Have you called the corporate office and asked to speak to him? Did you go to his apartment and see if the lights were on? Called his grandma or his personal assistant? Facebook stalked him?"

"No," I said.

"Why not?"

Marcie was right. She was almost always right.

I was way off my game here. This was basic stuff. Why hadn't I done it?

She seemed to read my thoughts and said, "You don't want to know the truth about Ty because you're afraid it will be hurtful. And, really, who can blame you? He's disappointed you so many times."

"You're right," I said. "You're right."

"Look at what's in front of you. Liam is a great guy. Don't let him get away while you're waiting for somebody who might never be there."

"He asked me out for our *soon* dinner, but I was busy. I haven't heard from him since," I said. "Now I'm wondering if he's changed his mind."

"He's probably just busy doing whatever it is lawyers do all day," Marcie said. "Maybe he's waiting for a sign from you? A little encouragement? Have you called him lately?"

"No," I realized.

Wow, I'm the worst sort-of girlfriend ever.

Marcie drew in a breath and said, "Look, Haley, you need to decide what it's going to be. If it's Ty, then you'd better find out what's going on with him. If it's Liam, then you should forget Ty and focus on him. It's not fair to keep Liam dangling."

Okay, now I felt like the most horrible sort-of girlfriend in the history of the entire world.

"I guess that's what I've been doing," I said. "I didn't realize."

"Hey, that's what best friends are for." Marcie

grinned. "Now, any more problems I can solve for you tonight?"

No way was I telling her about Jack now.

"Yes," I said. "I need a new dress to go with the new Mystique clutch."

"Me, too." Marcie downed the last of her soda. "Let's hit it."

Marcie and I didn't find new dresses we liked but, of course, that didn't stop us from buying other things. We hit Nordstrom, where I found some awesome jeans and a how-have-I-lived-without-it-this-long jacket, and she got some killer boots, two fabulous sweaters, and pants that were perfect for work.

Everything Marcie had told me tonight was circling through my head as we left the Grove, especially the part about how I wasn't being fair to Liam.

Not a great feeling.

I figured she was likely also right about giving him some encouragement, so I called him. His voicemail picked up.

Huh. That was disappointing. Here I was, ready to move things forward between us, and he didn't even answer his phone.

He was probably working.

Or maybe he was out with somebody else.

Crap.

I'd dealt with enough problems for one evening, I decided. I only had one more thing to handle, then I was going home, putting on my comfy pajamas, and breaking out my emergency package of Oreos.

I'd need them after dealing with Mom.

Traffic wasn't too bad as I took the surface streets to the 101, then headed north on the 2, and then east on the 210. My parents' place looked dark when I pulled into the circular driveway and parked.

Juanita must keep a constant vigil out the window because she opened the front door as I walked up. I held out the large envelope I'd picked up from the travel agent and said, "Would you give this to Mom?"

Yeah, I know, that was kind of bad of me but, jeez, I was running really low on emotional energy right now.

I desperately needed those Oreos.

"No," Juanita said, shaking her head. "You should go talk to your mother. She's in that room again."

Mom was seated on one of the big sofas in the media room when I walked in. The television was off and she was staring at the movie posters. I really didn't understand her sudden infatuation with Doc Brown and the 1950s gang in Hill Valley.

"Got your travel info," I said, and dropped the envelope on the sofa next to her.

I froze in horror.

She had on sweatpants and a T-shirt. Old, faded sweatpants. A stretched-out T-shirt.

Oh my God, where was my real mother?

"Mom, are you okay?" I asked.

"Of course, sweetie."

She picked up a glass of wine from the end table.

I relaxed a little. She was looking more normal now.

"Where's Dad?" I asked.

"Working late." She sipped her wine. "He's always working late."

"Courtney says she put together a great itinerary for you," I said.

Mom looked at the envelope for a moment, then turned away. "Good. Four months abroad is just what I'm looking for."

"Four months?" I might have said that kind of loud.

My parents took their share of vacations, but they'd never been away for that long.

"That's a really long time," I said, and managed to sound more reasonable. "Can Dad take that much time off from work?"

"Arrangements will be made," she said and finished her wine. She held the glass out. "Do ask Juanita to bring me another, would you, sweetie?"

I took the glass to Juanita—I didn't bother to tell her why, she already knew—and left. As soon as I dropped into my car, my cell phone chirped letting me know I'd missed a call.

Thank goodness. Liam had called.

The notion zapped me like a jolt from a shorted-out curling iron.

Yes, I really wanted to talk to Liam.

But when I dug my cell phone out of my

handbag, I saw Shuman's name on the screen. He'd left me a voicemail.

"We've had a break in the case," he said, when I checked his message. "We have a suspect in Asha's murder."

Chapter 10

I'd called Detective Shuman back right away last night, but he hadn't picked up. He'd sounded rushed in the message he'd left, so I figured he'd been working.

I checked my phone yet again as I hurried into the Holt's breakroom along with other employees reporting for our morning shift. Still nothing from him.

Jeez, what was going on? Shuman hadn't returned my call and neither had Liam. I still hadn't heard anything from Jack, plus I'd had no word on the delivery of the Mystique.

I stowed my handbag, fell in behind the other employees and clocked in, and checked the work schedule. I was assigned to the juniors' clothing department today. This was a stroke of good luck—which I really thought I was due for. It was the perfect location for me today because

I could crouch on the floor in front of the wall of jeans and use my cell phone unnoticed.

As everyone was headed out of the breakroom, the door flew open and Rita came in wearing red stretch pants and shirt with a herd—yes, an entire herd—of llamas on the front, each embellished with fringe and bejeweled eyes. Yet that wasn't the most unattractive thing about her.

She drilled us with majorly serious bitch-face.

"Listen up, people," she shouted. "Somebody blew it."

She glared at me.

Why was she doing that? I hadn't done anything—well, nothing that I thought she'd found out about.

"Somebody screwed up," she went on.

I hoped this wasn't about the mannequins.

No way am I doing new-hire orientation again.

"Somebody here at Holt's shot off their mouth," Rita said.

A murmur went through the group of employees, and everybody glanced around. I did the same, of course, just to blend in.

"Somebody spilled the beans about our store closing," Rita said. "Now that word is out, there might be more problems that Holt's doesn't want to deal with. News like this could keep customers away and affect sales, and that means everybody's hours could be cut back."

The store—and the employees—didn't need any more problems. Why would anybody—

Oh, crap.

I'd mentioned the store closing to Carrie at the bakery yesterday.

She'd told me she never paid attention to rumors. But, apparently, she'd jumped on this savory bit of gossip and spread it through the shopping center like breaking news of a blowout sale at the mall.

Okay, I could blame this on Carrie. Kind of.

"So if anybody from the other stores in our shopping center asks, tell them you don't know anything," Rita said. She pinned me with a nasty glare and said, "Everybody needs to keep their mouth shut. Everybody."

The employees filed out of the breakroom, and instead of straggling along at my usual place at the end of the line, I wormed my way to the front of the group and headed across the store. I wasn't about to hang around for any face time with Rita.

I reached the juniors' department and spent a few minutes pretending to size the pants on the jeans wall. The store officially opened for the day and customers began to roam the aisles. Luckily, shoppers in this department pretty much knew what they were looking for so I seldom had to actually interact with them. Still, I kept my gaze glued to the jeans and concentrated my efforts on looking like I was completely focused on the task.

From the corner of my eye, I caught sight of a customer moving straight toward me. Immediately, I turned my head and—yikes!—Detective Shuman was standing next to me.

I hadn't even heard him walk up. Was I losing my edge?

Shuman had on his slightly mismatched shirt-tie-jacket combo, indicating he was in cop mode. A wave of worry shot through me. In the phone message he'd left me last night he'd said he had a suspect in Asha's murder—I hoped that suspect wasn't me.

"Is this an official visit?" I asked, and managed to sound calm—at least, I hoped I did.

"I'm not arresting you," he said and grinned. "Not today, anyway."

"Where's Madison?" I asked, glancing around.

He nodded in the direction of the other shops in the complex and said, "We're still canvassing the stores, trying to contact everyone and follow up on some leads."

"You found a suspect?" I asked.

Shuman glanced around. I did the same, just so I'd look cool, too. A mother and daughter were checking out T-shirts at a nearby rack. I walked to the other side of the department. Shuman followed.

He lowered his voice and said, "We got a tip that Asha was having an affair with a married man who works in the shopping center."

Wow, I hadn't seen that coming.

"Where does he work?" I asked.

"Owner of the convenience store."

A few things clicked into place.

"Asha was here that day to see *him*. That's why she was out back. They were there together," I realized

"According to our witness, his wife had found out about the two of them."

"Oh my God," I said. "Maybe she saw them together, became enraged, and shot Asha."

Shuman didn't seem as excited about my I-have-a-great-theory moment as I was.

"It's too early to speculate. We still have a lot of ground to cover," he said. "We're running background checks on everyone who had access to the rear of the shopping center, conducting interviews, evaluating evidence, waiting for lab results, looking for witnesses."

That really was a lot to cover. No wonder he hadn't jumped on board my oh-so brilliant and totally unfounded the-wife-probably-did-it idea.

"What about the surveillance tapes?" I asked. "Did you see anything?"

"Lots of activity. Cars coming and going. Employees arriving, leaving. Delivery trucks unloading," Shuman said.

I knew the surveillance cameras at the rear of the Holt's store offered a very limited view of the area.

"Nothing helpful," I realized.

"Not so far," he said.

Shuman looked slightly weary. I couldn't blame him. Searching for clues and evidence apparently took a lot of time and patience.

I'd never make a good detective.

"If I hear anything, I'll let you know," I offered.

Shuman nodded and left.

I went back to the wall of jeans and started

sizing them again. They didn't need it, but it made me look busy in case a customer, or Rita, approached. It was mindless work, which was good because my brain was doing the hamster-on-a-wheel thing with the information I'd just learned from Shuman.

Was Asha's lover covering her rent on that expensive apartment and making the payments on her BMW? Was that how she managed to live in such luxury?

Not likely, I decided. Shuman had told me the lease was in Asha's name—her name alone. Apartment complexes didn't let anyone move in unless proof of sufficient income was provided to cover the rent. Same with her expensive car.

No way could she have swung those things on her minimum-wage jobs—or managed to sock away the fifty grand Shuman had learned was in her bank account. I needed to find out how Asha maintained her lifestyle and why she was leading a double life by pretending to be an average, minimum-wage gal.

Of course, Jack could have gotten that info for me, but I still hadn't heard from him.

I was definitely moving beyond slightly miffed with Jack.

Regardless of how Asha supported herself, she'd had an affair with a married man whose wife knew all about it—a tried and true motive for murder. I definitely needed more info on that whole situation.

It occurred to me then that I'd been way off base when I'd gone to Cakes By Carrie. Apparently, there was no connection between the bakery and Asha's death.

I caught sight of Rita talking to the clerks in the jewelry department across the aisle, so I dropped to the floor and started shuffling the jeans around.

I didn't feel so great about having upset Carrie with the news of Asha's murder. That whole thing had spun completely out of control, somehow. She'd gotten so upset I'd figured she and Asha had been good friends, yet, now that I thought about it, Carrie had never said that they were.

Had her off-the-scale reaction been genuine sorrow over Asha's death? Or had it been cover for something else?

Either way, her behavior was suspicious.

I added Carrie's name to the mental list of suspects I'd started, along with the wronged wife of Asha's love interest.

After several more minutes of moving the jeans around, I stretched up and saw that Rita was no longer in the jewelry department. I got to my feet and spotted Bella winding her way through the clothing racks toward me.

"Wrong hot guy," she said. "Not the cop hot guy, the other hot guy."

It took me a few seconds to remember that Bella had asked me if I was working with Jack on Asha's murder, in the hope that he would come into the store.

"Still, he's a good-looking man," she said, her gaze lingering in the direction Shuman had gone. "Perked up my day considerably."

Really, he'd perked up mine, too—except for the whole murder discussion, of course.

"Now, we've got to get the other hot guy in here." Bella leaned closer and lowered her voice. "I've been in stealth mode. Got some intel."

I hadn't really expected Bella to come up with anything, but I rolled with it.

"You need to go talk to Grace," she said. "Something went down between Asha and a customer the day before she got killed."

"Here? In the store?"

Bella nodded. "Grace said it got real ugly, real quick. An argument. She said it looked like they were going to throw down, then the woman walked off."

My senses jumped to high alert. Could this woman have been the wife of the man Asha was reportedly having the affair with?

"I'll check it out," I said. "Thanks."

I abandoned all pretense of working and went to the customer service booth. Grace was inside, at the inventory computer, looking up stock numbers for the bundle of returned dresses and skirts on the counter next to her. She dropped what she was doing and walked over.

I'd known Grace for a long time so there was no reason to finesse the topic with her. I came right to the point.

"I heard you saw Asha in the store the day before she died," I said. "Some sort of confrontation with a customer?"

"It was weird," Grace said. "One minute I was waiting on this woman, and the next she was in a shouting match with Asha."

"What about?"

"I couldn't tell, exactly. She'd already left my booth and, somehow, they saw each other right there by the T-shirts," she said and nodded to the display shelves in the women's clothing department. "It was something about Asha having the nerve to show her face here. The whole thing was pretty intense."

My this-is-a-major-clue antenna shot up.

"I don't suppose you remember the customer's name?" I asked.

"No, but she returned pajamas, those neon orange and yellow ones we got in right before Christmas, remember? Everybody's been returning those things," Grace said. "She didn't have a receipt, but she'd paid for them with her Holt's credit card, so I credited her account."

"Her info's in the computer," I realized.

I punched the code into the cypher lock on the customer service booth's door and let myself inside.

"So what's going on? You think this is connected to Asha's murder?" Grace asked as we walked to the inventory computer.

Suddenly I felt just like Shuman—which was way cool—reluctant to speculate or commit to anything.

"The timing is suspicious," I said.

"Cool."

Grace tapped on the keyboard and scrolled through several screens.

"That's her," she said. "Valerie Roderick."

I pulled out my cell phone and snapped a photo of the transaction.

"I'll let you know if I see her in the store again," Grace offered.

"Great. Thanks," I said.

I left the customer service booth. No way could I go back to the juniors' department right now. I pushed through the double doors into the stockroom.

Aside from the store's canned music track, it was quiet back here. The truck team had already come and gone. Boxes of new merchandise—baby clothes—were stacked in the receiving area. Some of them were open already, so I knew that the sales clerks who were stocking the department would return soon for another load. I dashed up the big concrete staircase to the stockroom's second floor and wound through the shelves to the lingerie section located in the back.

The info I'd gotten from Grace was basic stuff—Valerie Roderick's home address, phone number, and Holt's credit card info. I needed to find out if she was, in fact, the wife of the convenience store owner who was reportedly having the affair with Asha.

Of course, I could have simply called Shuman and asked him. But he was with Detective Madison canvassing the shopping center so, unless I just happened to catch him at the perfect moment, it was unlikely he could blurt out the info I needed.

Besides, I wanted to get this lead on my own, check it out, and deliver the info to Shuman fully formed and workable if I came up with anything.

And, of course, it never hurt to remind Shuman how cool I could be.

I Googled Valerie's name and followed a series of links that led me to her photo, confirmed her home address—it's really scary what strangers can find out about you on the Internet—and the shop she owned named Valerie's Vintage. It was a clothing store located not far from Holt's, near the mall.

The name of her shop was familiar, even though I wasn't into vintage clothing. I'd probably seen the place, since I was at the mall so often, but something else was going on with it.

Then it hit me.

I scrolled through my phone to Asha's résumé. She'd worked at Valerie's Vintage last summer.

Coincidence?

No way.

Chapter 11

By the time my four-hour shift ended, I was certain Detectives Shuman and Madison had finished canvassing the shopping center and talking to possible witnesses, and were gone. Now it was my turn.

I headed for the convenience store located at the opposite end of the center. Not much seemed to be happening there today. The parking lot at this end of the center wasn't even half full.

Most of the businesses had big signs in their windows advertising their January clearance sales. The craft store had filled two sets of rolling display shelves with Christmas wrapping paper, bows, and tags, positioned them on the sidewalk near their entrance, and marked everything down fifty percent. The mail center offered BOGO deals on shipping boxes that they'd stacked near their door. The furniture store wasn't offering discounts on anything—which proved the place was a drug front, if you ask me. Delightful aromas—though total opposites—drifted out of Cakes By Carrie and the cigar store.

As I walked past the craft store I caught sight of Carrie inside, talking to an older woman behind the counter. She was short and thin, with fried-out blond hair in the same style she'd probably been wearing since tenth grade. I'd never seen her before, but I seldom came to any of the shops in the Holt's center.

Carrie glanced out the door at that moment and we made eye contact. I started to give her a little wave, but she jerked away, leaned in, and said something to the woman, who then threw me a look and turned back to Carrie.

Oh my God, they were talking about me—and not in a nice way. How much more obvious could they be?

Carrie was probably telling the woman how I'd upset her with the news of Asha's death.

No way did I want to get involved with that whole thing again.

I kept walking.

A feeble little bell sounded when I entered the convenience store. The place was packed with all sorts of snacks, some staples, and a few household products. Refrigerator cases ran along the back wall. The front counter was near the entrance, backed by shelves of cigarettes.

I needed to find out what was up with Asha and the affair she'd had with the store's owner. Of course, Shuman and Madison had been here only a few hours ago and had covered the same ground. I figured that could work to my advantage—especially when I saw that the cashier on duty was considerably younger than me. She was short and slim with tats on both arms, a nose ring, an eyebrow piercing, and had gothed herself out in head-to-toe black.

I browsed through the candy section—just so I'd look like an actual customer, of course, like all the great undercover operatives—while the only other two people in the store paid for their sodas and left. Grabbing a Snickers bar, I went to the counter.

"Oh my God, Raine," I said, reading her name tag. "Can you believe what's going on in this place now? The cops were just in Holt's asking all kinds of questions. Were they in here?"

She glanced at the Holt's lanyard I'd left dangling around my neck and muttered, "Yeah," as she scanned my Snickers.

"So it's true?" I asked, adding a little gasp. "The cops really think the guy who owns this place is involved in that girl's murder?"

Raine rolled her eyes. "Owen. He's an idiot."

I managed to gasp again and said, "What? You don't think he did it?"

"Could have." She pointed to the total on the cash register. "That will be a dollar fifteen."

"Oh my God. He was having an affair with the murdered girl, for reals?"

"Yeah, going out back, saying he was having smoke," Raine said. "Please. How stupid does he think I am?"

The bell chimed over the door. A man walked

into the store. He headed for the refrigerator cases in the back.

"Yeah, that's bad," I said, and opened my handbag. "I mean, he was married, right?"

"Francine." Raine rolled her eyes again. "What a psycho. She's always in and out of here."

"So she knew about the two of them?" I passed her a five.

"Everybody knew," she said, and handed back my change.

"And that didn't stop them?"

"Like I said, Owen's an idiot. And Asha? I don't know what was up with her," she said. "I just put in my hours and leave."

I dropped my change into my handbag and grabbed the Snickers.

"Thanks," I said, and left the store.

I unwrapped the Snickers as I headed down the sidewalk.

At least now I knew that Owen's wife was named Francine, which meant she wasn't the Holt's customer Grace had seen arguing with Asha the day before she was killed. Still, there could be some sort of connection. Valerie Roderick and Asha wouldn't have had a near smackdown at Holt's for no reason.

My cell phone buzzed. Liam's name appeared on the ID screen. I got a pleasant little rush—and I hadn't even bitten into my Snickers yet.

"How's your day going?" he asked, when I answered.

Our relationship was too new for me to mention that I was looking for possible murder suspects, so I went with something that wouldn't likely cause him to break up with me.

"I just finished my shift at Holt's," I said.

"And now you're going shopping," he said.

Already, he knew me so well.

"How about dinner on Saturday night?" Liam asked.

I froze. Was this the dinner he'd mentioned when he'd come by L.A. Affairs? The special occasion for something he wanted to discuss? Oh my God, what could it be? Something wonderful, definitely. At least, I thought it would be something wonderful. Maybe I should downgrade it to something good. That way, I wouldn't be disappointed. But I really liked wonderful better than good. Or should I—

"Haley?"

"I'm here," I said. "Sure, dinner on Saturday night would be great. Where are we going?"

He knew what I was thinking because he said, "Wear something dressy."

Instantly, I mentally shuffled through my entire closet. I had nothing appropriate for the occasion, of course.

"How about seven?" he asked.

"Sounds perfect," I said.

A funny little warmth glowed inside me as we ended the call. I started in on my Snickers just to keep the good feelings rolling.

Now, of course, I had to completely rearrange my afternoon—which I was totally okay with.

As I headed for my Honda parked outside of Holt's, I dropped my planned visit to Valerie's

Vintage further down my mental to-do list and put buying a new dress for Saturday night with Liam at the top. I decided Nuovo would likely have the perfect dress for the occasion—plus, while I was there I could check on my Mystique clutch, which I knew would look awesome with whatever dress I picked out.

Yet all of that could wait.

First, I had to call Marcie and tell her everything.

I swung by my apartment and changed out of the dress-down-to-fit-in clothes I always wore at Holt's and into dress-up-to-impress pants and sweater so I'd fit in at Nuovo. I'd left a message for Marcie earlier. She finally returned my call—really, having a job when major gossip was going down could be so inconvenient—as I left my apartment and headed for Nuovo.

She was still at work but we discussed my upcoming evening with Liam from every possible angle—what we thought might happen, what should definitely happen, what could go wrong, what he might say, what I might say—all of which was, of course, total speculation. Still, it had to be done.

We also covered exactly what type of dress I should buy—length, neckline, color—and how I should accessorize it—minimalistic or flashy—and style my hair—down or up-do. We agreed that the Mystique clutch was a major must-have, absolutely the only bag that could properly finish my look.

"We were supposed to have them by now, weren't we?" Marcie asked, as I pulled into a parking space down the block from Nuovo.

"Something about a delay in the shipment," I said, as I got out of my car. "I'll find out what's going on."

"Send me pictures of every dress you try on," she said.

"Of course," I told her and ended our call as I headed down the sidewalk.

The day was gorgeous, as most Southern California days were, even in January. The afternoon sun was bright and warm, the sky clear, the breeze almost nonexistent. Lots of shoppers were out—women mostly, a few couples, and some moms pushing baby strollers. This place was sure busier than the Holt's shopping center had been.

A sales clerk stood near the register when I walked into Nuovo. Our gazes crossed and, instead of giving me the usual our-favorite-customer-just-walked-in reception, she turned and ducked through the curtain that covered the door to the stockroom.

Okay, that was weird.

Still, I wasn't going to let it bother me. Nothing was going to upset me right now. I had a big date coming up with a smoking-hot guy, I was buying a new dress and might possibly walk out of this store today with a look-at-me-and-be-jealous new handbag to carry for the occasion.

I glanced around the sales floor but didn't spot Chandra. It hit me then that the other clerk might have recognized me, known I was

Chandra's client, and gone into the stockroom to get her.

Two other customers were in the store looking at the jeans. I headed for the racks of dresses. I found three right away—all short, black, and sleeveless, yet distinctly different in a way only women can discern—and headed for the dressing room.

Voices from behind the curtained doorway caught my attention.

"What are we going to do? She's Chandra's client."

I was sure it was the sales clerk who'd disappeared when she saw me walk in. She sounded worried.

Not a good sign.

"Damn it," another woman—probably a sales clerk—replied. "Where is Chandra?"

"I have no idea. She's supposed to be here."

"Did she call?"

"No. What about her client? What am I supposed to tell her?"

I didn't need x-ray vision to see there was still a problem with my Mystique clutch bag.

"Hello?" I called, and managed to sound calm.

The clerks fell silent and, a few seconds later, the one I'd seen when I walked in glided through the parted curtains wearing an if-I-look-like-everything-is-okay-it-really-will-be-okay smile.

I wasn't buying it.

She spotted me and the dresses I was holding and said, "Hello, Ms. Randolph. It's so nice to see you again."

Like she didn't already know I was in the shop.

I wasn't buying that, either.

"Chandra isn't here today. I'm Kendal," she said. "Please allow me to assist you. Are you ready to try on?"

"What's up with my Mystique?" I asked.

"Oh, well, as I'm sure Chandra explained previously, there's been a delay in our shipment."

I had to hand it to her, she said it as if this were just a minor situation, soon to be resolved, instead of the catastrophic disaster that I suspected it really was.

Still, I remained calm.

"What kind of a delay?" I asked. "Was it late from the manufacturer? Delivered to the wrong address? What?"

"There's no need for you to trouble yourself with the details, Ms. Randolph," she said. "I assure you—"

"Tell me." I might have said that kind of loud.

Kendra shifted uncomfortably, glanced back at the curtained stockroom doorway, then drew herself up and said, "Actually, our shipment of Mystique handbags was . . . lost."

"Lost?" I definitely said that kind of loud.

Oh, crap.

Chapter 12

I probably should have stomped out of Nuovo in a full-blown snit-fit over the situation with my Mystique clutch, but come on, the dress I selected for my big date with Liam looked great on me and I got it at an eighty-percent discount.

We all have our priorities.

Even though Kendal had assured me that everything possible was being done to recover the lost shipment of Mystiques, I doubted a strike force was being assembled somewhere to locate a box of blue leather clutches embellished with peacock feathers.

I stopped by my Honda and stretched the garment bag containing my new dress—black, sleeveless, plunging, short—across the back seat. I would have to tell Marcie about what had happened with our Mystiques, but not right now. She was at work and, really, nobody should receive that kind of news without family or friends nearby.

My afternoon definitely needed a boost, so I locked my car and headed for the Starbucks located down the street. Even without the jolt of chocolate, sugar, and caffeine, my brain was spinning pretty fast, thinking about the missing shipment of Mystiques—and how I could still get one for Marcie and me.

Ty popped into my head.

Holt's owned Nuovo. Ty's family owned Holt's. He ran them both. Did he know the shipment had been lost? Could he pull some strings to get another order of the clutches sent to Nuovo, pronto?

Maybe I should call him and ask—though I should probably leave out the part about wanting to take it on a date with another guy.

Of course, for all I knew Ty was still on sabbatical, trying to sort out his life. I shouldn't intrude unless it's an emergency. But this was, after all, a shipment of designer handbags. Major bucks were involved. He would want to know, right?

I stopped at the corner and waited with other pedestrians for traffic to clear. Halfway across the intersection, the mental image of Ty seeing my name on his caller ID screen and not answering sprang into my head.

It made me feel pretty yucky.

When I stepped up onto the curb on the other side of the street, that image morphed into Ty, dressed in his business suit, answering his phone at his office downtown, where he'd been for weeks without bothering to tell me he was back in town.

I felt even yuckier.

Wow, I really needed a Starbucks now.

I walked past shop windows displaying mannequins dressed in gorgeous clothing, decked out in fabulous accessories, and it hit me—I wanted that Mystique.

My emotional turmoil suddenly whipped itself into an F5 tornado. I had to find out what was going on with Ty so I'd know if he could get that bag for me.

I pulled out my cell phone and called Amber, his personal assistant.

Amber and I had always been cool with each other, even after Ty and I broke up. I hadn't talked to her in a while so I wasn't sure what kind of reception I'd get. I was relieved when she answered right away.

"Oh my God, girl, how are you?" Amber said.

She was young, brunette-smart, and super organized. I'd never worried about her having a thing for Ty—not after I'd noticed her checking out Marcie's butt.

"Pretty good," I said. "What's up with you?"

"Just trying to stay ahead," she said. "No, he's not back yet."

I didn't bother pretending not to know she was talking about Ty or that I hadn't called to find out if he'd returned.

"I'm paying his bills, keeping up on his emails, and forwarding him the important ones," Amber said.

A wave of concern washed through me. Ty

really was off the grid—way off, and had been for months now. I wondered if something else was going on.

"Is he okay?" I asked.

"Seems to be. I hear from him regularly."

"Where is he? What's he doing?" I asked.

All sorts of ideas flooded my head.

Was he sequestered in a cabin high in the Himalayas, meditating and doing yoga? Trekking across Antarctica? Studying art and painting watercolors on the bank of the Seine?

Or living on a secluded beach somewhere with a hot chick?

"I've got no clue where he is," Amber said. "So what's up? Did you need something?

It seemed kind of selfish—even for me—to contact Ty after all this time just so I could get my hands on a fabulous purse. Still, I was willing to do it, but Amber spoke first.

"You want me to contact him, ask him to call you?" she asked. "You know, Haley, Ty would do anything for you."

That was nice to hear, but I wasn't so sure it was true.

"No, don't do that," I said. "I just . . ."

Just what?

In that instant, I wasn't sure what, exactly, I wanted to say to Amber that could explain my call to her. Sure, it was about the Mystique. But something else was going on. I knew because my heart had started to ache, my breathing had gotten labored, and heaviness had settled over me. Images of Ty filled my mind—how tall, strong, handsome, smart, generous, kind, caring he was—along with the big question I still couldn't come to terms with: Why? Why couldn't things have worked out for us?

"You're sure?" Amber asked. "I can email him right now. It's no problem."

Should I do that?

I was tempted—oh, wow, I was really tempted. But how long would it take to hear back from him? How many hours, days, or weeks, maybe, would pass while I jumped every time my cell phone rang, thinking it was him?

And what if it was *never*?

"Haley?"

The notion that he might not call me at all boiled down to a hard knot in my belly.

I'd spent enough time waiting for Ty.

I had to stop letting myself get all twisted up about him. We'd broken up. I couldn't put myself through this any longer.

"No," I said. "Never mind. It's no big deal. Don't mention my call to him, okay?"

"Sure, if that's what you want."

"It is," I said, and ended the call.

I headed for Starbucks.

While I sat at a table near the window sipping my Frappuccino, I decided to move Valerie Roderick to the top of my mental to-do list.

I wasn't sure what kind of reception I'd get from her at her vintage clothing shop. She had, after all, gotten into a heated argument with Asha in Holt's and was seemingly unconcerned about making a public spectacle of herself. Chances were good Valerie wouldn't take too kindly to me, a total stranger, waltzing into her shop, telling her I knew about her near throw-down, and asking about her involvement with her former employee who was now a murder victim.

Go figure.

While I finished my Frappie, I did an Internet search for Valerie and her shop. I'd already done some preliminary work but thought it prudent to dig deeper in case she had an arrest record, a history of violence, or something else I should know about.

Valerie's Vintage had a cool website featuring a wide variety of women's clothing and accessories. There were lots of photos depicting racks and display units crammed with merchandise. It ranged from vintage designer fashions to items that seemed to be just old stuff that I figured she'd bought at a yard or estate sale which, technically, I suppose, was still considered vintage.

According to the site, the shop had been around for about three years. Valerie must have been knowledgeable about both vintage clothing and managing a business if the place had been up and running for that long. Small shops—especially those aimed at a niche market—weren't easy to keep above water.

I followed a number of the links but didn't discover much more than I had on my initial search. No news reports about Valerie being a psycho who'd shot up her own business, or disgruntled customers throwing bricks through the windows, or a protest staged in front of her shop over alleged inhumane use of cotton-blend fabrics, or anything else that could be dangerous to walk in on.

No need for me to arrange backup before going in.

After finishing my Frappie, I strolled down the street and turned the corner onto Theater Drive. Valerie's Vintage was situated between an Italian restaurant and a toy store. It had a large display window featuring headless mannequins dressed in layers of chic fashions from different eras, old wooden chests bursting with scarfs and jewelry, and a bureau with open drawers overflowing with sweaters and blouses.

When I went inside, Valerie—or her decorator—had continued the retro vibe with black and white prints of Chanel evening gowns, Hermès dresses, and Halston sheaths framed on the walls. The place was quiet. I didn't see any customers or sales clerks. Nor did I see a lot of merchandise, contrary to their website photos, which showed displays crammed with fashions. This store was hardly the first to fudge a bit on its website. I wondered, though, if this was an indication that business had fallen off and Valerie had been forced to let Asha go. Was that why she'd left last summer? Or perhaps Asha had quit, having grown weary of spending hours, days, weeks, and months confined in this small shop.

I could totally relate.

Whatever the reason, Asha's departure hadn't been a smooth one, apparently, given the argument Grace had witnessed in Holt's. Something was still festering between them, all these months later. If I was lucky, maybe it had led to murder and I could solve the case today.

I mean that in the nicest way, of course.

There were, thank goodness, no handbags to distract me, so I checked out the clothing while waiting for Valerie to appear. I found an awesome pair of orange and yellow plaid hip-hugger bell-bottom pants that some hot chick must have totally rocked back in the seventies. There were dresses with shoulder pads that I was certain had been strutted by ladies in the grips of the who-shot-JR mystery, complete with panty hose, pumps, and chunky jewelry. I got a History Channel Woodstock documentary flashback seeing the psychedelic peasant blouses and love beads.

I wandered to the jewelry display spread out on the glass case near the cash register. I wasn't into vintage but, wow, these pieces looked awesome. Right away I spotted earrings that would look great with the dress I'd just bought, then I saw a necklace, a bracelet, a—

"May I help you find something?"

I jumped at the sound of a woman's voice and whirled around. Valerie stood behind me.

Oh my God. I was definitely going to have to work on my stealth-mode skills.

I recognized Valerie from her photo online—late thirties, tall, dark hair, pleasant looking. She had on a pink sleeveless, belted dress that was probably in style during the first moon landing.

"I love these earrings," I said, and held up the pair I'd picked out.

"Are you thinking of pairing them with that?" Valerie asked, indicating the bracelet I was also holding.

I took a closer look. It was a chain bracelet embellished with crystals and coral roses. Gorgeous, but now that I'd taken a closer look, I realized it was not really me.

"It looks like my mom."

In any other shop that comment might have come across as insulting, but Valerie rolled with it.

"Then maybe you should get it for her," she suggested.

Buy a gift for my mom for no special reason? Why hadn't I ever thought of that before?

"It's Prada," Valerie pointed out. "Ceruse crystals. From their iconic coral rose 2012 collection."

I saw the Prada logo engraved on the clasp, so I knew it was the real thing—well worth the three-hundred-dollar price tag I discreetly glanced at.

Valerie waited while I draped the bracelet around my wrist and turned it left, then right, studying how it looked and imagining it on Mom.

"She'd love it," I said.

Valerie still didn't say anything, didn't push for the sale, which I appreciated—and which was probably the reason she'd stayed in business all this time. Small shops lived or died by their reputation. Nailing a customer with heavy-handed buy-it-now pressure didn't inspire return business.

Mom had been really upset the last time I'd seen her over that whole back-in-the-day beauty pageant scandal involving her second-place finish in the Miss Whatever-it-was competition. Even though she was over it now and planning a long vacation, I figured it wouldn't hurt to surprise her with a gift. And wasn't Prada the perfect pick-me-up?

"I'll take it," I said.

"How about the earrings?" Valerie asked.

If I could buy my mom a gift, I could certainly get one for myself.

"I'll take them, too," I said.

Valerie took the jewelry and moved behind the counter.

"Shall I gift wrap the bracelet?" she asked.

"That would be nice," I said.

Valerie made quick work of boxing the items and wrapping the bracelet in antique blue paper and ribbon. Then she tapped on the cash register and gestured to the displayed total.

Four hundred and fifty bucks. Not a lot, considering what I'd purchased, but sizeable enough to put it on my credit card.

"Does your mother shop here?" Valerie asked.

"I don't think so," I said, as I dug my wallet out of my handbag—a terrific Fendi tote. "But after she sees this bracelet, I'm sure she'll want to come by and check things out for herself."

I flipped through the cards in my wallet—driver's license, auto club, medical insurance, Macy's gift card, but no Visa from the Golden State Bank & Trust.

What the heck?

I went through everything again, looked in the other slots in my wallet, and dug to the bottom of my tote. The card wasn't there.

Oh my God. I always kept that card with me. Had I lost it? Or worse—had it been stolen?

Was somebody running from store to store throughout Southern California, racking up charges in my name? Or website hopping, ordering extravagant luxuries that I would be billed for?

Why hadn't my bank called me? Why hadn't I gotten an alert? I'd signed up for that service, hadn't I?

I sensed Valerie staring.

Okay, this could have been really awkward but, luckily, I had a don't-get-embarrassed-at-check-out backup plan in place. I pulled out my emergencies-only MasterCard and passed it to Valerie.

She chatted about something but I couldn't listen. I was in semi-panic mode.

When had I last used that credit card? I thought back. I hadn't purchased anything in a while, except for the dress at Nuovo, which I'd used my debit card for. I didn't remember charging anything—

Then it hit me.

I'd used it the night Marcie and I had dinner together, at the restaurant just down the street, the night I'd ended up in Jack's bed—which I absolutely could not think about right now.

Maybe I'd left the card at the restaurant. I'd check. Then I'd search my car, my apartment, the handbag I'd carried that night. I'd ask Marcie. Maybe she'd picked it up by mistake.

I thought hard, trying to come up with another spot to search. If I couldn't think of more possibilities that meant—

Oh my God, had I left it at Jack's place?

Oh, crap.

Chapter 13

"Thanks," I said, taking the small shopping bag from Valerie.

"You're very welcome," she said. "I know your mom is going to love that bracelet."

I smiled and headed for the door.

Wait. Hang on. I couldn't leave yet. I'd come here to question Valerie about Asha's death.

I've really got to do better about staying focused.

I oh-so-cleverly pretended to get distracted by a rack of acid-washed jeans with zippers at the ankles, and glanced up to see that Valerie had come from behind the counter sensing, I'm sure, another possible sale.

I waited until she got close, then said, "Asha McLean used to work here, didn't she?"

Valerie froze. Her I'm-always-helpful smile curdled.

Oh, yeah, I was definitely onto something here.

I decided to hit her with the big news and see what kind of reaction I got.

"She's dead, you know," I said. "Murdered."

I got a small gasp and a double blink from Valerie but nothing more, nothing that indicated she was surprised to hear the news, or that she already knew.

After a few more seconds, Valerie said, "Well, I can't say I'm shocked."

"Why's that?" I asked.

Her eyes narrowed a bit, and she said, "How do you know Asha?"

"We worked together."

Valerie drew back a little like I'd suddenly started to stink. "Where?"

She must have known Asha had worked at a lot of places, since she'd seen Asha's résumé when she'd hired her, so this should have been a logical question. But Valerie looked angry, suspicious, like something else was going on.

"At that website of hers?" she demanded.

Website? What website?

"At Holt's," I said. "Asha ran a website?"

Valerie's expression morphed from anger and suspicion to just plain old anger.

"That so-called review site of hers." Valerie all but spit out the words. "That Exposer site."

I'd never heard of an Exposer site, but I wanted to keep Valerie talking so I rolled with it.

"Oh my God, Asha ran that?" I asked. "You're kidding."

"I wish I were," she told me, then waved her

arms around. "Look at this place. My business has fallen off to nothing since she posted that horrible review. I'm still trying to recover. And it was lies she told—lies."

"Asha deliberately posted things that weren't true?" I asked.

Valerie fumed, now seemingly angry at herself. "I hired her. I believed her. I fell for her story about wanting to learn the retail business from the ground up, and working her way toward a business degree. And all the while, she was really nosing around my shop, uncovering every tiny troublesome situation that arose, every miniscule problem, and blowing it up into a major catastrophe that she included in that review of hers."

"So what she reported was true?" I asked.

"Yes, some of it was, but she blew it completely out of proportion, made it into something it wasn't," Valerie said. "And she fabricated other things that had no basis in truth."

"Why would she do that?"

"Money, of course," Valerie told me. "That site of hers is vile and mean-spirited, and for some reason, she has thousands of followers."

People loved bad news. They flocked to places that reported it which, in turn, attracted lots of advertising revenue.

I didn't doubt what Valerie was saying but, really, how much damage could one bad review really do?

"So Asha wrote an unfavorable review," I said. "And you think that one thing was the cause of your business troubles?"

Valerie's anger rose again.

"Twitter blew up," she told me. "Tweets were flying. Claims were made that my designer fashions were knockoffs, that I bought clothing from sweatshops overseas, that I was contributing to child slavery."

"And none of that was true?" I asked.

"No!"

I took a step back.

Valerie's face turned a deep red. "*Los Angeles Magazine* was going to do a story on my shop, but they cancelled!"

Okay, I was kind of afraid of Valerie now.

"Even some of my family and friends believed those lies and turned against me!"

Maybe I should have brought backup.

Valerie drew in a breath and let it out slowly, trying—hopefully—to calm herself.

"The whole thing has been a nightmare," she said. "A nightmare that won't end."

I felt bad for Valerie, that her shop had fallen victim to what she claimed was—and what seemed like—a malicious attack. Looking around the place, I could see that business wasn't good. Asha and her website had, apparently, done a great deal of damage to the shop's reputation.

"Is that what you two were fighting about at Holt's the other day?" I asked.

She was so wrapped up in her own thoughts and anger, she didn't seem to wonder how I'd found out about the argument.

"I couldn't believe she had the nerve to walk up to me, to show her face, and actually ask how my shop was doing," Valerie said. "She didn't fool me. I knew she was up to her old tricks, getting hired somewhere, learning the ropes, then sensationalizing and lying about what went on behind the scenes."

"Asha worked at Holt's for a few weeks last fall," I told her. "She quit just before Christmas."

"You look at her site. You just look at it," she said. "I'll guarantee you there's a scathing review about Holt's."

Holt's was a major international corporation. I doubted that anything Asha wrote could have been detrimental to business in a significant way. Still, I didn't like the idea of her making up lies or embellishing difficult situations to attract readers and generate more ad money.

Valerie seemed to wind down a little more and said, "I'm not the least bit sorry Asha is dead. It sounds as if she got what she deserved."

Honestly, it sounded that way to me, too.

And it sounded like Valerie had an excellent motive for murdering her.

Valerie had been super wound up so I decided to check out Asha's website and see for myself what, exactly, she'd posted. Honestly, I wasn't expecting anything as devastating as Valerie had described. I mean, really, how bad could the review of a clothing store be?

As tempted as I was to hit Starbucks again, I didn't—even I have my limits, occasionally. I stopped on the sidewalk outside the Italian restaurant next door to Valerie's Vintage and did a search on my cell phone. I found Asha's site right away.

Yikes! The recent reviews she'd posted about a vacuum cleaner store and a candle shop were beyond scathing. They were downright mean, vile—way beyond a simple reporting of the facts. They read more like a tell-all exposé.

I typed *Valerie's Vintage* into the search box and the review popped up. When I read it, I actually gasped aloud—it was *that bad*, just as bad as Valerie had indicated.

A few follow-up comments had been posted defending the shop, but tons of other commenters had piled on, supporting Asha's accusations that Valerie's merchandise was all overpriced knockoffs, and making it sound as if Valerie were single-handedly to blame for forced child labor overseas and deplorable sweatshop conditions.

If Valerie really had murdered Asha, I didn't blame her. I'd have wanted to kill Asha, too.

I scrolled through reviews of other businesses that Asha had posted, going back for nearly a year. There were dozens of them, all horrific, and all of them had incited comments similar to what Valerie had endured.

I was dismayed to see that some businesses had taken out ads on Asha's site. I knew that companies had to go where the customers were, but why had they paid good money to be a part of something so awful?

I left the Exposer site and pulled up the photo I'd snapped of Asha's résumé, then cross-referenced her employment history with the reviews. She'd worked for many of the businesses. It seemed that Valerie was right—Asha had taken jobs to gain inside knowledge, then used it to write scathing reviews. She'd deceived the people who had hired her, she'd no doubt lied to her co-workers—she'd even gone so far as to drive that beat-up old Chevy for cover.

Cakes By Carrie flew into my head. I searched the Exposer site and, sure enough, Asha had ripped up the bakery with claims of unsanitary conditions, low-quality ingredients, and lost orders.

Unlike in Valerie's case, this tell-all review of Asha's—with its follow-up snarky comments—didn't seem to have unduly damaged Carrie's bakery, at least not from what I'd seen of the place. This struck me really fortunate—or something. I wasn't sure what.

Really, almost everything about Carrie seemed a bit odd to me.

When I'd been in her bakery and given her the news that Asha was dead, she'd seemed genuinely surprised. Was that true? Or was she putting on a show for my behalf?

After the horrible review Asha had done of the bakery, I'd have thought Carrie's reaction to the news would have been similar to Valerie's—relieved, almost glad, certainly happy that justice, in a way, had been served.

But Carrie hadn't seemed to feel that way.

Perhaps, unlike with Valerie's shop, the review hadn't really done that much damage to the baker's reputation, so Carrie wasn't all that concerned about the things Asha had said about her shop.

Or maybe Carrie had known all along that Asha was dead because she was the one who murdered her. One thing was clear—lots of business owners had a motive for killing Asha.

The info I'd uncovered today was definitely good stuff, so I decided I should let Detective Shuman know so he could factor it in with everything else he'd learned about Asha—and so he could be impressed with my awesome detecting skills, of course.

I sent him a text message asking if he could meet me. With the schedule he kept, or the lack thereof, I never knew when he was available or when he was too involved with a case to pull himself away, but he texted me right back saying he'd be there in an hour.

So that left me with some time to kill. I looked around at all the shops, stores, and the mall entrance just a few blocks away. Oh, yeah, I could occupy myself, no problem.

Then it occurred to me that the way my awesome detecting skills were rolling today, maybe I could find my lost credit card.

First, I accessed my account online. No charges that I hadn't made had been posted—whew! I still hadn't gotten an alert from GSB&T about suspicious activity on my account, another good sign. Hopefully, this meant I'd simply misplaced the card and I could still find it somewhere.

A little oh-please-let-this-be-easy tremor rumbled through me as I headed for the restaurant down the block where Marcie and I had met earlier in the week—the one where Jack had shown up and—and—and, well, I still couldn't remember what had happened after that.

I couldn't think about it right now.

Inside the restaurant, I approached the hostess stand. The place was getting busy with the dinner rush but she took the time to check the lost and found in the manager's office, then returned with regrets. I thanked her and left.

After dashing off a quick text to Marcie asking if she'd somehow ended up with my Visa, I went to my car and checked under and between the seats, but didn't find it. Marcie texted back a few minutes later stating she didn't have my card.

At this point, there was nothing to do but go shopping.

I headed for Macy's.

After an hour of sampling makeup, trying on shoes, and combing the handbag department in the hopes of spotting a Mystique clutch—there wasn't one—Detective Shuman texted me. He'd just pulled into the parking garage. I left the mall.

It was dark now, so the twinkle lights in the shrubs and trees had come on. Music floated from the hidden speakers. I spotted Shuman turning the corner, headed my way. His tie was pulled down and his collar was open. I doubted he'd had as leisurely a day as I had.

When he got closer and saw me, he grinned.

Shuman's got a killer grin.

"I had a feeling I'd hear from you," he said.

Obviously, there'd been a tremor in The Force.

"Did you find Asha's killer?" I asked.

"Did you?"

Shuman was still in detective mode even though he was, apparently, off work for the day.

Okay, if he wanted to play it that way, so could I.

"I found a whole bunch of suspects," I told him.

His eyebrows rose. "Yeah?"

"Yeah."

We stared at each other for a few seconds.

"Buy you a beer?" I asked, and nodded down the block.

Shuman shook his head. "I don't have time."

"Meeting Brittany?"

He grinned, but in a different way—which was still totally hot.

"You might as well tell me what you found out today," I told him. "If I had a date tonight, I'd have already blabbed everything to you and been gone."

Shuman frowned. "Did you break up with Liam?"

"We're seeing each other tomorrow night," I said. "Come on."

I led the way to one of the benches situated on the plaza and we sat down.

"What did you find out?" I asked.

Shuman didn't answer.

"You can't keep Brittany waiting," I told him.

He still didn't say anything. His I'm-not-talking-first cop training was really irritating at times. Obviously, he'd learned something significant in his investigation. If he didn't soon tell me, I might have to beat it out of him.

I could take him.

I'd have to blindside him, of course.

"Okay, fine," I said, and huffed a bit just so he'd know this didn't quite suit me, then filled him in on what I'd learned about Valerie's Vintage and Asha's Exposer website, plus the argument between Valerie and Asha that Grace had witnessed at Holt's.

He listened intently and nodded occasionally. I even got a slight eyebrow bob once, indicating that this was news to him.

I gave him a minute or two to think about everything, then said, "Can you believe companies actually advertise on that site?"

"At least now we know where all of her money came from," he said.

"Asha lived really well," I said. "She must have charged a lot for those ads. I still don't get why any reputable business would want to be associated with a site like hers."

"Small businesses are desperate," Shuman said. "They have to reach customers wherever they can."

He was right, of course, but the whole thing still didn't sit right with me.

"Did you learn something today that ties in with this?" I asked.

"We got a hit on the background checks we were doing on the employees who work in the shops next to Holt's," Shuman said. "Seems a woman who owns one of the stores shot and killed her husband last year."

"*What?*"

"It was ruled an accident," he said. "The handgun was inside her purse and when she reached inside, it went off. The bullet struck and killed her husband."

"Oh my God, that's awful."

Shuman shrugged in a way that made me think he didn't share my feelings.

"You don't think it was an accident?" I asked.

"She knew how to handle a firearm. She had a license to carry concealed," Shuman said. "It was a thirty-eight, the same caliber as the weapon used to kill Asha."

"Coincidence?" I asked.

"Maybe." Shuman shook his head. "But I don't like it."

"So who is she?" I asked.

Shuman hesitated.

"Look, I work in that shopping center. I visit those other stores," I said. "If there's a woman there who *accidentally* shot her husband, I want to know who it is."

"Dena Gerber," he said. "She owns the craft store."

I remembered seeing Carrie talking to her when I'd walked past the craft store. I'd been sure they were talking about me.

"Did you get the gun from her for a ballistics check?" I asked.

"No probable cause. We've found no connection between her and the victim—yet."

"Maybe you have now."

I grabbed my cell phone and looked at the photo I'd taken of Asha's résumé, but didn't see the craft store listed as one of her previous jobs. I accessed the Exposer website, hoping I'd find a scorching review that would make Dena Gerber another suspect. Nothing.

"Or maybe not," I admitted and put my phone away. Still, I wasn't ready to give up on Dena Gerber as a suspect so I said, "Maybe she's some sort of Black Widow? Has she had a lot of husbands? Have they all turned up dead under mysterious circumstances, maybe?"

Shuman shook his head and said, "She was married once before, divorced years ago. Husband number one was alive and kicking at the time."

"Did you interview the girl who owns the bakery?" I asked. "Cakes By Carrie?"

Shuman thought for a few seconds and said, "Carrie Taylor? Nothing seemed out of the ordinary. No red flags, no alarms. Why?"

"Asha wrote a terrible review about her bakery," I said. "I don't know. I just get a weird vibe from her."

He rose. "Let me know if your vibe turns up some hard evidence."

"You'll look into Valerie Roderick?" I asked. "She had a really strong motive for wanting Asha dead, plus they had that argument at Holt's."

"I'll check into it," he promised.

"Have fun with Brittany."

Shuman grinned and left.

I sat on the bench, thinking. Seemed I now

had a long list of suspects—the wife of the man at the convenience store who had reportedly had an affair with Asha; Valerie Roderick and everyone else who'd been skewered by the Exposer website; Carrie; and now Dena Gerber.

Of course, it would be easier to come up with the murderer if I had some evidence to go along with the motive I'd uncovered.

I headed down the sidewalk toward my car, running all sorts of scenarios through my brain—all completely trumped up, at this point, since all I could do was speculate on what might have gone down the day Asha was killed.

I needed more information—and I wasn't all that sure how I'd find it.

Chapter 14

"Something's going down," Bella murmured.

I followed her oh-so subtle eyebrow bob across the racks of clothing in the women's department. Saturday morning and the store was crowded, but I easily spotted a group of six men and women trooping down the hallway that led to the training room and managers' offices.

They looked like they were definitely on a mission.

"Hey, that's the slimeball from the convenience store," Bella whispered. "Owen something or other. Always hitting on me when I go in there."

"Which one?" I asked.

"The one with the Donald Trump combover."

I spotted him immediately, trailing along at the back of the group. I figured him for late forties, short, soft looking, and kind of pudgy. Not exactly the kind of guy you'd imagine Asha—half his age—having a fling with. Owen must have had something going for him that wasn't readily apparent, though, honestly, I didn't want to think too hard about what it might be.

"See that old guy in front? The tall one?" Bella said. "He owns the furniture store."

He was old, all right. His snow-white hair was combed straight back. He wore a crew-neck sweater and what I'm pretty sure was a leisure suit. He'd completed his look with two gold chain necklaces and a pinkie ring. He was either mobbed up, or stuck in the seventies—or maybe both.

"You ask me, that place is a drug front," Bella told me.

I spotted Carrie in her bakery uniform. Dena was behind her. I didn't know the other man, but guessed he ran the cigar store.

None of them looked happy.

"What're they doing here?" Bella asked.

"This can't be good."

I wound my way through the racks of clothes, Bella on my heels, and watched as all of them disappeared into Jeanette's office.

"Something is definitely going down," Bella said.

Jeanette's door closed with a thud.

Not a good sign.

"At least it's not those people from corporate," Bella offered.

I cringed slightly as Ty flew into my head. I pushed him out.

"What's going on?"

Sandy appeared next to us.

"The owners of the stores in the shopping center just crashed Jeanette's office," Bella said.

"Maybe it's a surprise party for Jeanette," Sandy said. "You know, for her birthday."

"I don't think so," I said.

"That would be cool, wouldn't it?" Sandy said.

"I'm pretty sure it's not a surprise party," I said.

"My birthday is next week," Sandy said. "Jeanette and I could have been born on the same date."

I gave up.

"What are you doing for your birthday?" I asked.

"That boyfriend of yours better be planning something special for you," Bella told her.

"Actually, he is," Sandy said.

Bella and I shared a this-is-seriously-doubtful look.

"Really, he is," Sandy insisted. "He already told me. He's taking me out to dinner, someplace nice. It's going to be romantic, I just know it."

Honestly, I wasn't convinced. Sandy's boyfriend was a world-class jackass as far as I was concerned. He treated her terribly. I really hoped he'd come through for her on her birthday. She deserved it—and a lot more—for everything she'd put up with from him.

"You'll see," Sandy told us.

I hung around the women's department pretending to straighten the clothes so I could keep an eye on Jeanette's office. Whatever was going on in there couldn't be good—and it was taking a long time. Finally, the door opened and the center's business owners trooped out again.

Nobody looked any happier than they had going in.

I waited, thinking Jeanette might come out and I could *just happen* to see her and ask what was up. She didn't show. I was tempted to go ask her flat-out—I'm not good at holding back—but I heard an announcement over the PA system paging the assistant manager on duty to Jeanette's office. Apparently, she needed backup for whatever was going down.

Really not a good sign.

Bella appeared next to me looking grim and said, "Now what's going on?"

"I don't know," I said.

But I was sure we'd find out sooner rather than later—and it definitely would not be good for us employees.

When my shift ended at Holt's, I headed out the 210 to my parents' house to give my mom the bracelet I'd bought for her. I hadn't heard from Juanita or anyone in the family with reports that Mom was still upset over the Miss California Cupid gossip that was making the pageant rounds, so I figured I could be in and out quick—always the best way to visit my mom.

Besides, my big date with Liam was tonight and I had a ton of things to do. Marcie was joining me for a mani and pedi. Even though we'd discussed the outfit I'd selected, my accessories, and how I'd do my hair and makeup, we would, of course, have to cover everything again—which was half the fun of going on a big date.

We were both still speculating on what the evening really meant. Liam hadn't told me where we were going, only that I should wear something dressy, which I interpreted as expensive and romantic. Was I right? Did he want a spectacular setting to discuss our relationship, or to break some big news to me? Or had he simply found a fabulous place to dine that he wanted to share with me?

I was feeling pretty darn good about life as I exited the freeway, wound through the hills, and parked in the circular drive outside my folks' home. Juanita met me at the door, looking somewhat grim.

"Your mother, she's in that room again," she told me.

I waved away her comment. No way was I getting mired down in any sort of situation. I had too much to do.

I headed through the house, fishing the gift-wrapped bracelet from my tote—a terrific Prada—planning a quick drop-off and an even quicker escape. After all, I had a mani and pedi appointment. Mom, of all people, would understand.

The lights were dim when I walked into the media room. The television wasn't on. No music played.

Mom sat on the sofa wearing a—oh my God, she had on her bathrobe.

Now, granted, it was a La Perla silk robe that my dad had purchased for her last Christmas to the tune of five hundred bucks from Neiman Marcus, but if my mom was still in her bathrobe in the middle of the afternoon, something was definitely wrong.

"Mom?" I walked closer.

A few seconds passed before she looked at me.

"Oh, hi, sweetie." She managed a small smile. "You look so nice today."

I had on my Holt's-wear, jeans and a crappy sweater. And Mom thought I looked nice?

"Did you hit your head, Mom?"

Her gaze drifted away and finally returned to me.

"You know, Haley, I was always so disappointed in you," she said.

I just looked at her.

"You remember how you never liked dancing or singing or modeling?" she asked.

Like I could ever forget those nightmares she'd put me through?

"All those lessons I took you to when you were little," Mom said. "I tried so hard to find something you were good at."

Jeez, how many more hurtful things could she hurl at me?

Mom shook her head. "I was so hoping you and I could connect, that we could share a love for those things. I wanted us to be close."

Okay, this was totally weird.

"Are you sure you didn't hit your head, Mom?" I asked.

"I wanted us to do mother-daughter things."

"Shortness of breath, maybe?"

"I wanted us to share a special bond," she said.

"Weakness on one side?"

"But we didn't," she said. "Still, you turned out so wonderful."

Mom grew quiet and gazed across the room. A few minutes passed before it finally sunk in that, after her initial comment, she'd said a really nice thing about me.

"I brought you something," I said, and held out the gift.

She looked up at me, then at the gift. "Oh my goodness, what a delightful surprise."

Mom patted the sofa and I sat down beside her. She took her time opening the package, then lifted out the bracelet.

"It's . . . it's beautiful."

She burst into tears.

Oh my God, what was going on? I went into semi-panic mode. Something was majorly wrong with Mom—she was crying while she had on *silk*.

"Things don't always turn out how we think they will," she sobbed. "Or the way we want them to."

I rifled through my tote, found a travel pack of tissues, and stuffed all of them into her hand. She drew in a ragged breath and choked back her tears.

I had no idea what was going on but thought this was a great time to move the conversation in a different direction.

"You must be excited about your European

vacation," I said, and forced a big see-now-we're-happy smile.

"I've rethought the vacation," Mom said, and dabbed at the corners of her eyes. "I've decided we should move."

"Oh, well, okay," I said. "You know, I've always imagined you living in Bel Air, or Beverly Hills. Hancock Park, maybe."

"I'm thinking of Montana."

"Montana?" I'm sure I said that kind of loud.

Mom nodded. "Or Sri Lanka, maybe."

Sri Lanka? I wasn't even sure Mom could find Sri Lanka on a map. Why the heck would she want to live there?

Obviously, something else was going on with her, something that had nothing to do with a European vacation, moving out of state or leaving the country, or my dislike for singing, dancing, and modeling lessons as a child—which meant, thank goodness, none of this was my fault.

"Okay, Mom, you have to tell me what's really going on," I said.

She pressed the wad of tissues to her lips and turned away. I thought I was going to have to pry it out of her, somehow, but then I realized she was looking at the *Back to the Future* movie poster again.

Was that the problem? Did she want to go back in time?

We all did, at some point. Who didn't wish they could change something in their past? Maybe not stay so long at a bar and drink too much wine, then wake up the next morning in a strange bed, unable to remember maybe having hot, sweaty, jungle—

Oh my God, I was thinking about Jack.

Mom sniffed, bringing me back to the moment.

Was she missing her pageant days? The competition? The camaraderie backstage with other contestants when she was young, when she had no husband or children, no responsibilities?

Then it hit me.

"This is about that Miss California Cupid pageant, isn't it?" I said.

My question seemed to galvanize her. She gave her nose on final swipe and sat up straighter.

"Of course not," she insisted.

No way did I believe her.

I always tried to be Switzerland where Mom was concerned and not get involved or take sides, but I couldn't remain neutral on this one. She had totally flipped out and had gotten worse every time I saw her. Something had to be done.

I couldn't imagine my aerospace engineer dad digging up pageant dirt, or my student/model sister knowing where to begin to look. My brother, even if he weren't in the Middle East, would be useless.

That meant it was all me.

I was going to find out just what the heck had gone on at that beauty pageant, and put an end to the gossip.

Chapter 15

Liam had selected a place on Melrose Avenue, a well-established restaurant for L.A.'s well-heeled. The atmosphere was subdued, quiet conversations broken only by the clink of heavy silver flatware, crystal, and bone china. Dark wood and snowy white linens were set aglow by candlelight.

The chef's menu with a wine pairing ran about three hundred bucks a person. I was totally up for the fabulous meal—my idea of cooking was making a sandwich and toasting the bread.

Liam looked especially handsome tonight in a navy-blue Canali suit that perfectly complemented my black-sleeveless-plunging-short dress. Only the Mystique could have made the look better, but I was really okay with the Kate Spade envelope clutch I'd selected.

"Let's have a drink before dinner," Liam said

after the maître d' assured us our table would be ready shortly.

"I'll join you in a minute," I said.

I slipped down the darkened hallway toward the ladies' room. Liam had gone all-out for the evening, so no way did I want to sit across the table from him through the entire meal only to later excuse myself to the restroom and realize I'd looked like a complete idiot the whole time with lipstick on my teeth or a tendril of hair sticking straight up.

Just as I reached the door to the ladies' room, the men's room door opened. Jack Bishop walked out.

We both froze.

I hadn't seen him since *that night*. He hadn't called, texted, or emailed me. He hadn't come by my apartment or either of the two places I worked. He'd made no attempt to contact me at all.

Now we were standing face-to-face. What was I supposed to say? How was I supposed to act?

Jack's gaze took a long, slow dip from my head to my feet, and up again.

He was thinking about that night—I knew he was. Why wouldn't he? Obviously, unlike me, he actually remembered what had happened.

"No Mystique?" he asked.

I'd told him about the clutch I wanted? Yeah, okay, that seemed kind of familiar.

"Nuovo's shipment was lost," I said.

Jack grinned. "It wouldn't have mattered. You look great tonight."

And I hadn't looked great *that night*?

Had I fallen asleep with my mouth gaping open? Had I snorted in my sleep—or worse?

Jack edged closer. He had on a charcoal-gray Tom Ford suit that looked fantastic on him, and wow, he smelled great. The crazy heat that always rolled off of him seemed hotter tonight.

"Are you and Marcie out again?" he asked.

Okay, this was kind of awkward.

"No . . . no, I'm with. . . ." I glanced back down the hallway and gestured lamely at Liam in the bar.

When I turned to Jack again, his expression hardened into something between anger and hurt.

"You're with Liam Douglas?" he asked.

I wasn't surprised Jack recognized Liam. Jack consulted for a number of businesses in Los Angeles, and many of them were law firms.

"Are you?" Jack asked again, and sounded none too happy.

I'm a real stickler about being involved with only one guy at a time. This wasn't a great moment for me.

"I know how this looks," I said, "me being out with Liam after what happened the other night."

One of his eyebrows rose. "After what happened?"

"You know, between us," I said.

Jack just looked at me.

"At your place," I said.

He seemed to lapse into deep thought, glanced away, then looked at me again.

Oh my God, he was remembering everything

we'd done—whatever it was. I wanted him to say something, give me some hint of what had gone on, but he didn't.

Crap.

"I hope you know I'm not like that," I said. "I had too much wine and, well, things just . . . they got out of control."

"You know, I usually get a thank-you," Jack told me.

A thank-you? Women usually thanked him after spending the night at his place?

I knew it. Jack was so hot he didn't just scream his own name—he probably spelled it out.

I couldn't take any more of this conversation.

"Look," I said. "The whole evening just got crazy, or something, I guess."

Jack frowned. "You don't remember?"

How insulting to tell him I didn't remember—and it didn't make me look so hot either. So what could I do but lie?

"Of course, I remember," I said.

Jack eased closer, and a grin pulled at his lips. "So you remember us having . . . ?"

Jeez, why did he put me on the spot like this?

"Hot, sweaty jungle sex," I told him.

A huge, knowing smile bloomed on his face.

Oh my God, I'd had hot, sweaty jungle sex with Jack and I couldn't remember it?

Nooooo . . .

A hand touched my back and Liam appeared next to me. I was so rattled, I couldn't say anything—I couldn't even think.

Luckily, I didn't have to do either. Jack and

Liam did the whose-is-firmer handshake, and were in the middle of some age-old male posturing when the maître d' showed up and escorted us to our table.

The evening had just begun and I was exhausted.

Fortunately, Liam didn't ask anything about Jack. Since he was a lawyer, he was a good talker. He always had something to discuss, a witty or clever story to share. Tonight I was having a little trouble staying focused, so I was shaken a bit when, just before dessert was served, Liam reached across the table and took my hand.

"Would you consider going away with me for the weekend?" he asked.

We'd been going out for a while now, taking it slow—really slow—so I'd known this situation would eventually present itself. I'd already thought about it. I liked Liam, really liked him, so the idea of going away with him for the weekend didn't come out of the blue, yet on the heels of that conversation with Jack, it didn't seem right.

A night with Jack, then a few days later, the weekend with Liam? I knew it sounded old-fashioned, but I'm not that kind of girl.

But Jack hadn't asked me to go away for the weekend. He hadn't invited me anywhere. I'd apparently had hot, sweaty jungle sex with him, but he hadn't bothered to call me afterwards.

"I'd love to go," I said.

"What do you think?" Sandy asked, holding up her cell phone for Bella and me to see.

We were in the Holt's breakroom snacking on vending-machine fare, all of us fiddling with our cell phones while we talked. Around us, other employees were microwaving their lunches, shoving in empty calories and sugary drinks, everybody grinding through our morning shift until we could clock out and get on with our actual lives.

Bella and I studied the selfie Sandy had taken in a dressing room where she'd tried on a pink maxi-dress.

"Is it big-birthday-dinner worthy?" she asked. "I'm not sure."

"That boyfriend of yours is really taking you out?" Bella asked. "For reals? No b.s.? He's really doing it?"

"He promised," Sandy said and smiled her he's-so-adorable smile. "He can be really sweet like that."

Bella and I exchanged a he'd-better-do-this glance.

"Sometimes he doesn't always come through," I pointed out, as gently as I could—well, gently for *me*.

"He's busy," Sandy said insisted. "His work is important. He's always in demand."

"He does tattoos," I said.

"It's art, Haley," Sandy said.

Jeez, how many times had we had this conversation?

"The dress looks great on you," I said.

Sandy took another look at the selfie on her phone and said, "Yeah, I'll wear it. He'll like it."

"You want me to do your hair for your date?" Bella asked.

Her geometric-shapes phase continued. Today she'd fashioned her hair atop her head into a giant rectangle that looked a bit like a waffle iron.

Sandy thought for a few seconds, then said, "I think I'll wear it down. He likes it when I wear it down."

"Do you know where he's taking you for dinner?" I asked.

"He won't tell me," Sandy said. "He says he wants to surprise me. He sounds very mysterious about it."

It sounded to me like he hadn't made a plan yet, but I let it go and took a quick glance at my cell phone.

I'd accessed my Visa account on the GSB&T site and was relieved to see that there were still no unauthorized charges on my card. It had been days since I'd realized it was missing which, hopefully, meant that, despite the careful search I'd already done, it was somewhere in my car or apartment, or something, and not stolen, so I could still find it. I didn't want the hassle of requesting a replacement since GSB&T processing on everything could be timed with a sundial.

"You remember that guy I told you about, the one I started dating a couple of weeks ago?" Bella asked.

Sensing major gossip, I set my phone aside. Sandy did, too.

"The IT guy at the insurance company?" I asked.

"How's it going with him?" Sandy asked.

"He's hinting around about having a sleepover at my place," Bella said. She shook her head. "I don't know. He's nice, but he's not all that great looking. I don't know what to do."

"What's your lighting situation?" I asked.

"Bright."

"Is he worth investing in low-wattage bulbs?" I asked.

She shook her head. "I'll just break up with him."

"You should give him a chance," Sandy said.

"I haven't got time for that kind of b.s.," Bella grumbled.

A blinding wall of red, orange, and yellow flashed in the breakroom doorway. Just as I was about to duck and cover, I realized it was Jeanette walking past.

"I've got to go," I said, jumping up from my chair.

Bella looked at me as if I'd lost my mind. I couldn't blame her—I was only twenty-two minutes into my fifteen-minute break.

"Later," I whispered, and gave her a something's-going-down eyebrow bob. Bella got it immediately and bobbed back.

I dumped my trash, pocketed my cell phone, and left the breakroom.

The door to Jeanette's office was open so I headed that way. She didn't usually work on Sunday so I knew something major had to be happening.

I stopped in the doorway and grabbed the door frame to steady myself. Jeanette stood behind her desk wearing a dress with neon red and orange flames streaking upward on a yellow background. It had a round collar and capped sleeves, and I was pretty sure it was made of velour.

It looked like it was old enough to vote.

"Yes, Haley, what is it?" she asked.

It took everything I had, but I managed not to shield my eyes as I walked up to her desk.

"Are you doing okay?" I asked, and actually sounded concerned, not just nosy. "You've looked kind of stressed lately."

Jeanette sighed and sank into her desk chair. She hadn't invited me to join her, but I sat down anyway. I mean, really, you have to push a little if you want to hear the good stuff.

"All the owners of the adjoining shops came to see me," Jeanette said. "They're very unhappy about our latest situation."

I was sure "situation" was code for "murder."

"Sales are down. Business is off. Customers are staying away in droves," she went on.

"Even here?" I asked.

"We're definitely feeling the effects," Jeanette admitted.

I couldn't help but think the *effect* she was most concerned about was the impact on her quarterly bonus.

"Things are much worse for the smaller businesses," Jeanette said. "Most of them are barely getting by."

"So why did the owners come to you?"

"They think I'm to blame for their problems because the body was discovered here."

Jeanette cut her gaze to me and I got a definite this-is-really-*your*-fault vibe.

I decided it was better not to say anything.

"The police haven't made any headway in finding Asha's murderer. Those investigative journalists are coming," Jeanette went on. "If this thing isn't cleared up soon, giving the reporters something positive to say, the whole shopping center could go down."

The content of a television broadcast and the police finding a killer quickly were both highly unreliable things on which to pin the future of the entire shopping center.

"There must be something else that can be done," I said.

"The other business owners expect Holt's to make things right," Jeanette said.

"How?"

"Corporate is working on some ideas."

I didn't feel encouraged.

And I was definitely going to have to step up my efforts to find Asha's killer.

Chapter 16

It was a Louis Vuitton day. Definitely a Louis Vuitton day. Was there a better way to start a Monday morning?

I sat at my desk in my office at L.A. Affairs, dressed in one of my fabulous business suits—black, with carefully selected take-me-seriously yet look-at-me-I-have-great-style accessories.

Since I was coming in only a few days each week until things picked up, I had a number of clients, vendors, and venues to check on. Likely there would be a few fires to extinguish, wrinkles to iron out, and problems to get a jump on. So the first thing I did—after catching up on the office gossip and getting coffee in the breakroom, of course—was call Marcie.

She'd been occupied with a family function over the weekend—Marcie had a great family—so I'd texted her with only the basics of my dinner with Liam on Saturday night. I'd left out the part about seeing Jack at the restaurant. Even though Marcie and I were the best besties ever, I still couldn't bring myself to tell her what had happened with him.

"A quaint B-and-B in the mountains," Marcie said. "I had no idea Liam could be so romantic."

"Me either," I admitted.

Liam had definitely impressed me with his getaway plans. Ty had taken me to super-nice places, including Europe, but all of our trips had revolved around business. He'd been gone a lot, leaving me to occupy myself, and had been distracted by problems that had to be dealt with immediately—

I sat forward in my desk chair. Why was I thinking about Ty? I didn't want to think about him. In fact, I'd decided *not* to think about him. What was the matter with me?

"When are you going?" Marcie asked, thankfully bringing me back to our conversation.

"Weekend after next," I said.

"Oh my God, you have to go shopping soon," Marcie told me.

While I'd displayed a woeful lack of natural talent during the singing, dancing, and modeling lessons Mom had subjected me to as a child, I'd demonstrated some mad skills during skiing and ice-skating sessions. The closet in my second bedroom was packed with all the necessary winter gear and equipment—which was no reason not to go shopping for something new.

"I need boots, definitely some boots," I said. "And sweaters."

"We'll check out Nordstrom," Marcie said.

"They're having a sale on coats. You should think about getting a new coat."

I didn't have to think about it; I was getting one.

"We'll go one night this week," Marcie said.

"I'll text you," I promised, and we ended the call.

Since I'd just had a mani and pedi a few days ago, I didn't need to book a spa service. I had nothing Facebook-worthy to post. I'd already checked my bank account and Visa card twice this morning. All of which meant there was nothing left to do but get to work.

I spent the morning talking with venues and vendors for my clients' upcoming events, making sure everything I'd already put into place was moving forward as expected. Then I contacted each client—or their personal assistant—and let them know I was on top of everything, and followed that up with an email to Priscilla, the office manager, informing her of pretty much the same thing.

Yes, I'm actually good at this job.

By lunchtime I'd done everything that required my attention—at L.A. Affairs, anyway. I left the office, got my car from the parking garage, and headed for Studio City.

This thing with Mom and the Miss California Cupid beauty contest was weird—beyond weird, really. I still didn't get why she was upset about the gossip that was circulating, to the point that she was talking about leaving the country.

Of course, nobody wanted their accomplishments to be tarnished, and Mom had a special place in her heart for that particular pageant. But she'd placed second. It wasn't like she'd been declared the winner and would lose a first-place crown if an investigation resulted in a full-blown shake-up.

This was hardly the first time I hadn't really understood what was going on with Mom.

I turned into the shopping center near Ventura Boulevard, parked, and went inside the travel agency where I'd picked up Mom's itinerary. I needed to get a handle on this thing, and I figured a good place to start was with her former pageant buddy, Courtney.

The office was quiet. Two of the agents were on the phone, another had an elderly couple seated in front of her desk.

Courtney spotted me, smiled, and waved me back.

"What a nice surprise," she said, shuffling some papers to the side. "I wasn't expecting you, Haley."

"I just need a minute of your time," I told her and dropped into the chair in front of her desk.

"Sure, no problem. Did Caroline have a question about the itinerary? She could have—" Courtney stopped and shook her head, looking totally mystified. "I can't get over how much you remind me of your mother—though not as much as your sister does, of course."

Like I hadn't heard that at every family gathering, holiday, and special occasion, from every family member, old friend, and stranger on the street since the day Mom and Dad brought my sister home from the hospital?

"It's uncanny, really," Courtney said, her gaze searching every angle and curve of my face.

I definitely had to change the subject.

"Were you in the Miss California Cupid pageant with Mom?" I asked.

"No, I met Caroline the year after that," Courtney said.

She seemed to get lost in pageant thoughts for a minute, then snapped out of it and gasped.

"Oh, dear, are you talking about those nasty rumors that are going around?" She made a decidedly un-pageant-like face. "Personally, I don't involve myself in that kind of thing. I don't read about it or talk about it, but I do, of course, hear about it from time to time. I can't believe the things people are dredging up these days, about something that happened a long time ago."

"Why would anybody care about it after all these years?" I asked.

"Well, for one thing, we former beauty queens are all very close. Pageants are very bonding experiences, you know," Courtney said. "So, of course, reputations are at stake, especially since the Miss California Cupid contest was a local pageant."

Mom involved herself in all sorts of community and charity events. I could see that she wouldn't want to be associated with questionable conduct right here in her own backyard.

"No one wants to be part of a contested crowning. It looks bad on everybody," Courtney said.

"Do you think the rumors going around are actually true?" I asked. "There was some sort of conflict of interest going on with one of the judges?"

She leaned closer and lowered her voice. I, of course, leaned in too.

"These things can be very political. Favors are often exchanged," she whispered. "It's not right and it's not fair, but it's true."

I couldn't disagree.

"Any idea what this conflict of interest was about?" I asked. "Or who the judge was?"

Courtney shook her head. "Like I said, I don't involve myself in the details of this sort of thing. Too negative. Life's too short."

I couldn't disagree with that, either.

But I did wish Mom felt that way, too.

"Thanks for your time," I said and rose from my chair.

"No problem," she told me. "And tell Caroline to call me. We need to have lunch."

"I will," I said, and left.

I got in my Honda, wishing that Courtney had given me a solid lead or at least some insider's info about this conflict of interest involving the pageant. Since that hadn't happened, I was going to have to find it the old-fashioned way—you know, actually work at it.

But right now I had a more pressing matter to look into—Asha's murder investigation.

According to the last conversation I'd had with Jeanette, the fate of the entire shopping center rested on uncovering Asha's killer. I'd come up with a number of suspects, and Detective Shuman had provided an is-this-weird-or-what coincidence with Dena Gerber's supposed accidental shooting of her husband. I'd also discovered more than one motive for Asha's murder.

Lots of puzzle pieces, but none of them were coming together to form a complete picture yet.

I pulled out my cell phone and accessed the Exposer website. The site was so mean-spirited, so hurtful, so destructive, I couldn't help thinking it had to be the jumping-off point for Asha's murder.

Scrolling through her posts over the past year or so, I was hit again with the sheer number of possible suspects. It wasn't just the owners who likely had it in for Asha, but their spouses, families, employees, and suppliers as well. A failed business affected lots of other businesses. Checking out all of those people was more than I could manage—at least in time to solve the murder before those investigative journals showed up at Holt's to do their story.

Then I realized there was a work-around I could try.

I clicked on the home page of the Exposer site and looked at the advertisements. The biggest one was a top banner from an auto repair shop, a place called Wright's Auto Works.

It still made no sense to me why any business would put its ad on this kind of site. Maybe if I found out more about the place and its owner, I could make some headway on the investigation.

Yeah, okay, it was a thin lead, but the only viable one I had to work on at the moment.

I clicked on the ad, got the address from the website, punched it into my GPS, and took off.

Wright's Auto Works was off the 134 on San Fernando Road in Glendale, set amid a stretch of similar businesses—a tire store, used car lots, an upholstery shop. Their parking lot was almost full when I pulled in. The garage had two bays, both of them with their doors up and cars on the racks. Several men dressed in Dickies work clothing, a standard uniform of dark trousers and a pale blue shirt with a name patch over the pocket, were busy in the bays.

I spotted a guy holding a clipboard and walked over.

His name was George, according to his shirt, and, according to the website, he was the owner. Even without the name tag I would have known he was running the place.

George was on the high side of forty, slightly overweight, balding, with the pinched expression and the sheen of forehead sweat of a stressed-out guy who had a lot to lose—and was, evidently, losing it.

"Hi," I said, favoring him with my I'm-really-nice-so-feel-free-to-tell-me-everything-I-want-to-know smile.

George didn't smile back. He glanced at his watch, his clipboard, then my Honda.

"What does your car need?" he asked.

"Actually, I wanted to chat with you about your advertising," I said.

He gave my awesome business suit and Louis Vuitton satchel the once-over, then shook his head.

"I'm not interested in buying any more advertising," he told me and walked away toward the garage bays.

I did look pretty darn professional. I could see why he'd mistaken me for a sales person.

"I'm here about your ad on the Exposer website," I said.

George froze, then spun around. His face turned beet red, his nostrils flared, and he bared his teeth.

Oh, crap.

"Get the hell off of my lot!" he screamed.

Oh my God, what was going on?

"I just wanted to ask you—"

"Go!"

What was wrong with this guy?

He took a step toward me.

I backed up.

"Don't you ever come back here again!" he yelled.

A mechanic walked toward us carrying a big wrench. Whether he intended to come after me, or George, I didn't know.

I wasn't about to hang around and find out.

I jumped in my Honda and sped away.

Chapter 17

I was totally rattled when I left Wright's Auto Works. Luckily, I found a Starbucks right away and calmed myself with a massive infusion of chocolate, sugar, and caffeine, as I headed north on the 5.

What the heck had come over George? Why had he become so enraged when I'd mentioned the Exposer site? It wasn't like Asha had given him a bad review; plus, he'd actually forked some serious cash to advertise with her.

His actions were so out there, so out of proportion, I figured something major was going on. I needed to find out what it was, but I definitely needed backup to go there again.

The image of Jack Bishop sprang into my mind. He'd be perfect to go with me, of course, but I was still kind of miffed with him over what had happened between us. I mean, really, he hadn't contacted me since our night together, and he'd actually had the nerve to tell me women usually *thanked him*?

Still, I had to find out what was up with Wright's Auto Works, and Jack was the guy to handle it. Besides, this was business. Just business. Nothing personal.

I called Jack as I transitioned onto the 14. The call went to voicemail so I left a message. Hopefully, I'd hear from him soon.

My evening shift at Holt's was looming, so I hit the Carl's Jr. drive-through, then stopped by my apartment and changed into jeans and a sweater. I couldn't bring myself to take my Louis Vuitton satchel into Holt's, of all places, so I swapped it for a Betsey Johnson and headed out.

The store was kind of quiet when I walked in, not unusual for a Monday night. Still, I couldn't get my conversation with Jeanette, and her concern that business had slowed for everyone in the shopping center, out of my head. I really hoped the corporate office would come up with something that would restore faith in the businesses and bring customers back.

"Oh, Haley, I'm glad you're here. Look at this," Sandy called, as I walked into the breakroom.

She was in line at the time clock, bouncing on her toes and waving her cell phone. I stowed my handbag in my locker and got in line next to her.

"I need your opinion. What do you think?" she asked. "Do you like this one better? I can't decide."

I looked at the selfie on her phone, another shot of her in a dressing room somewhere, this time wearing a black cocktail dress.

"This is for your birthday dinner?" I asked. "What about the pink maxi you'd picked out? I liked that one on you."

It was definitely Sandy, much more so than this cocktail dress.

"I think it makes me look too young," she fretted, and scrolled through the photos to present me with the one of her in the pink maxi. "See? I look young, don't I?"

"You are young," I pointed out.

"Yes, I know, but I don't want to look young—not too young," Sandy insisted. "Which one do you think he'll like best?"

Really, I couldn't have cared less which dress her idiot boyfriend might like best, but no way would I tell Sandy that. She was super excited about her birthday dinner, and I didn't want to ruin it for her.

"He'll love you in either one," I told her.

A big, dreamy smile bloomed on her face. "You're right. He will. He's so sweet like that."

"Which one do you like best?" I asked.

She flipped between the photos for a moment, then said, "The pink one. It's my favorite."

"Then go with that one," I told her.

The line moved forward and we clocked in. On the schedule above the time clock, I saw that I was assigned to the housewares department tonight while Sandy was needed in juniors. It looked like I had an evening of folding dishtowels and aligning place mats ahead of me.

"Thanks, Haley," Sandy called as we left the breakroom.

I made my way to housewares at the back of the store. Bella was already there unloading a U-boat of new merchandise, dozens of tablecloths and napkins in Barney purple and Big Bird yellow.

I hoped this theme wouldn't carry over into the women's spring clothing line. No way did I want to see Jeanette dressed in those colors. I might really have to quit.

There's only so much I can take.

"How's it going?" I asked, grabbing a stack of tablecloths from one of the packing boxes.

"Quiet," Bella told me. "This place has been like a morgue lately. Just because that girl went and got herself killed behind our building, that's no reason for customers to think—"

She gazed past me, completely enthralled with something, then sighed and moaned, "Lord, have mercy."

I turned and saw Jack walking toward us.

Oh my God.

He looked smoking hot dressed in jeans, a dark shirt, and a leather jacket. His hair was slightly tousled and he had a hint of a beard.

Maybe it was my imagination, but I swear he was doing that slow-motion walk like in those men's cologne commercials.

"You got a brother?" Bella asked.

Jack grinned and shook his head. "No brothers."

"Damn."

He turned to me. "You called."

I had? Oh, yes, I had.

I headed for the stockroom. Jack followed me through the double doors. We stopped in the bedding section, which, I swear, was simply because it was a convenient spot.

"I went by an auto repair place and—"

"You really don't remember what happened that night?" Jack asked.

Good grief. Not this.

He moved closer. I backed up and bumped into the shelving unit stuffed with pillows.

"Nothing? Nothing at all?" he asked.

Oh my God, he was using his Barry White voice. I'm totally helpless against a Barry White voice.

Jack braced his arm against the shelf by my head and leaned down. Heat rolled off of him.

"Maybe I can jog your memory."

He touched his lips to my cheek.

Wow, that felt great.

"Does this seem familiar?" he whispered and brushed his fingers across the back of my neck.

It didn't—but who cares?

"Maybe this will bring back something."

Jack kissed me. I mean, he really kissed me. Just when I thought I might melt into a puddle on the floor, he stepped back. The playful look I'd seen on his face a minute ago was gone.

He left the stockroom.

I collapsed against the shelves of pillows.

Oh my God, what had just happened?

It took a few minutes for me to pull myself together and realize I hadn't asked Jack about going to Wright's Auto Works with me. Great. Now what was I going to do?

Bella stood by the U-boat unloading boxes when I walked out of the stockroom. Jack was nowhere to be seen.

"What did you do to him?" Bella demanded.

"Nothing," I said.

"He looked none too happy leaving here," she told me. "You should have made out with him."

I kind of did—but only *kind of*.

"Are you okay?" she asked. "You're acting weird. What's the matter with you?"

Good question.

"I'll be back in a minute," I said, and headed across the store.

By the time I reached the breakroom, I still hadn't calmed down. I couldn't figure what the heck had gotten into Jack.

Then I decided it was better if I didn't think about him anymore tonight.

I called Shuman. His voicemail picked up so I left a message asking him to meet me later tonight after my shift ended. I needed somebody to go with me to Wright's Auto Works, and since no way was I calling Jack again, Shuman was it.

As I left the breakroom, Jeanette came out of her office. I was still so rattled after being with Jack in the stockroom I wasn't even fazed by the black and brown color-blocked pantsuit she had on.

That's how rattled I was.

"I'd like to hire you," she told me.

Obviously, I wasn't the only one who was whacked-out tonight.

"You already did," I said.

"Come into my office."

I followed and we sat down at her desk.

"The marketing department at the corporate office has come up with a brilliant idea to draw customers back to our shopping center," Jeanette said.

I braced myself.

"We're going to have a festival in the parking lot," she told me. "I've already proposed it to the other business owners, and everyone is on-board. There will be deep discounts on merchandise, and special promotions. We'll have entertainment, food, and fun things for kid and adults."

Corporate had come up with that? I was surprised.

I wondered if Ty knew about the problems at the shopping center. Would he have given the green light to the festival? Or would he have—

Oh my God, I was thinking about Ty again. But not really. This was business related. It had nothing to do with me caring about him, or thinking about how he looked and smelled, and always—

I gave myself a mental shake.

Jeanette's words had turned into blah-blah-blah, but I caught up.

"It's the best way to get customers in, showcase merchandise, and demonstrate to the public that the center is a safe place to shop," she said.

"When are you doing it?"

"This weekend."

I sat up straighter. "This weekend? How are you going to pull all of those things together in just a few days?"

"That's up to you," Jeanette said. "You're in charge of the festival."

Oh, crap.

"I know you also work as an event planner, so this should be a snap for you," she said. "The corporation will officially hire L.A. Affairs, giving you access to your contacts there. Someone from marketing will set up everything first thing in the morning so you can get on this right away."

I just sat there, my mind spinning. How the heck was I going to pull off an entire festival in such short notice?

"The investigative journalists will be here this weekend also," Jeanette said.

And I was supposed to perform this miracle for viewers of TV, cable, satellite, the Internet, and YouTube? With the reputation of Holt's and the other shops hanging in the balance?

"We're all counting on you, Haley," Jeanette. "The future of the shopping center is in your hands."

Great. Just what I wanted to hear.

* * *

My evening definitely needed a boost.

After my shift ended at Holt's, I headed for my favorite Starbucks near my apartment. Shuman had texted me back earlier and agreed to meet me there. So, on the drive over, I'd called Nuovo, hoping that maybe—just maybe—the lost shipment of Mystique clutches had been found.

No such luck. Chandra was full of apologies and told me again how anxious all the clerks at Nuovo were to finally see a Mystique in person, and that she'd contact me the minute the shipment was located and delivered.

That meant it was all up to Shuman to boost my evening.

I swung into the Starbucks parking lot and spotted him seated inside. I could see that, as usual, he had a coffee in front of him and a *venti* mocha Frappuccino waiting for me.

So far, so good.

Shuman smiled when I walked in. He stood up, and pulled out the chair for me.

"I hope you have some good news," he said, as we sat down.

Darn. Not exactly what I wanted to hear.

But his collar was open and his tie was pulled down. He looked tired. I figured I didn't look so great myself, after the day I'd had. That was the cool thing about Shuman. We were okay with each other no matter what.

I took a long drink of my Frappie to fortify myself, then said, "I had a scary run-in with somebody today."

I filled him in on what had happened with George at Wright's Auto Works. Shuman shifted to somewhere between cop-mode and I'll-kick-his-butt-for-you mode, leaning forward and looking slightly puffed up, angry, and concerned.

It was totally hot.

"I'm fine. Really, I'm okay. Nothing serious. But, honestly, I was kind of scared," I told him.

Shuman took a few seconds to consider what I'd said, then pulled out a little notepad from his inside jacket pocket and wrote down the pertinent info.

"It made no sense," I said. "It was like he completely lost his mind. There was no reason for him to turn on me like that, which makes me think something more is going on with him."

"I'll take care of it," he said, and tucked the notepad away. "I took another look at the background check we did on Carrie Taylor. She opened her bakery last spring. Before that, she had a string of jobs, broken by long stretches of unemployment. She last worked for a grocery store. No record. No firearm registered to her. No red flags or alarm bells went off."

"But Asha worked for her at the bakery and wrote that horrible review about her shop," I said. "They're connected."

"Stretch that connection to include murder and we'll have something." Shuman sipped his coffee and said, "I dug into Owen Bailey's past. Seems he's got a revolving door of employees at that convenience store of his, and he's had flings with a few of them. Asha was one of many."

If I'd had maybe-this-is-a-big-break antennae, they would have shot straight up and wiggled.

"Do you think Owen's wife finally had enough?" I asked. "Asha happened to be the one that drove her over the edge?"

Shuman gave me a maybe-so shrug. "The wife has no alibi for the time of the murder."

"Is there any evidence to tie her to the murder?" I asked.

"Not so far," he said and sipped his coffee again.

"What about Valerie Roderick?" I asked.

"Not a happy lady," Shuman said. "She had it in for Asha, which she freely admitted."

"What about an alibi for the time of the murder?"

"She gave one." Shuman frowned. "I'm checking it, but so far, things aren't adding up."

A little wave of anxiety rolled through me. I liked Valerie. She'd been done majorly wrong by Asha. I could see how she might have been pushed too far. I hoped she hadn't compounded her problems by killing Asha.

"I spoke with the detective who handled the Dena Gerber shooting," Shuman said.

"Did he think there was something fishy about it? Like maybe it wasn't really an accident that her gun went off and it just happened to kill her husband?" I asked.

"There was nothing to prove it was intentional."

"So the fact that the same caliber gun was used to kill Asha is just a coincidence?" I asked.

"Apparently," Shuman said. "Plus, there's no motive. Asha never slammed Dena's craft store on her site."

We sat there for a few minutes, neither of us saying anything. Shuman hadn't come up with new info that would point to Asha's killer. I'd made no forward progress finding her murderer, only uncovered more unanswered questions.

I'd have to dig harder—and put on a festival.

Chapter 18

"Haley?"

I heard the office manager call my name as I left the breakroom with my first cup of coffee and headed down the hall. Even though I was at L.A. Affairs, my Holt's training kicked in and I started walking faster—it was really early, okay?

"Haley?" Priscilla called again. "Haley!"

Crap.

Obviously, she wasn't going to give up like the customers did.

I stopped and turned back, and saw her striding toward me. She was mid-thirties, tall, and blond, and always dressed in chic fashions, as required. This morning, she looked like she was already on some sort of mission.

"Oh, Priscilla, good morning," I said, as if I hadn't heard her call my name over and over.

"I could see you were deep in thought, and I

can't blame you," she said, catching up to me. "After what you've done."

I'd done something?

I couldn't get a read from her expression on whether I'd done something good, or something I hadn't thought I'd get caught at.

"You've pulled off quite a coup," she told me.

Okay, it must have been something good. I had no idea what it was, so all I could do was give her a let's-see-where-this-is-going smile and wait.

Priscilla didn't disappoint.

"I got a call first thing this morning from the Holt's Department Store marketing department. They have a huge event coming up, and they asked for you specifically." An oh-my-God smile bloomed on her face. "You've landed us a major international corporation!"

Obviously, she'd never been into a Holt's store. Still, I was happy to take the credit.

"I'm always on the lookout for new clients," I told her.

I wasn't, but this sounded better.

"You must have worked some marketing magic to land them," she said, still smiling and looking oh-so impressed with me.

I saw no reason to mention that I worked at Holt's part-time, or that I'd been run over with the job of staging their festival.

Priscilla frowned. "They are insisting on a quick turnaround time on this. I forwarded you the marketing department's email detailing the event. Now, you'll have to be sure to—"

"I've got this, Priscilla," I told her.

She gave me a concerned look, and I gave her my don't-question-the-master look right back. What else could I do?

The last thing I wanted was for her to assign someone to help me who might learn that I worked at Holt's—not to mention that the owner was my former official boyfriend.

That might sully my accomplishment.

"Fine," she said, looking relieved. "But if you need help with anything, anything at all, let me know immediately."

"I will."

"And if any problems arise—"

"I'll handle them."

Priscilla took a few seconds to digest this, then said, "Good job, Haley. You're a true asset to us."

I went into my office, closed the door, and collapsed into my desk chair.

Oh my God, how was I going to pull this off?

I could have dissolved into complete panic mode, but I pulled myself together because, really, I could handle this.

This was a slow time of the year, not only for L.A. Affairs, but for our vendors as well. I knew it wouldn't be a problem to book pretty much whoever I needed for the Holt's festival this weekend. Even if I had to resort to my B-list of vendors, I knew that would work in my favor, too. They'd knock themselves out for L.A. Affairs and would do a superior job hoping to get bumped up to my A-list.

Gulping down my coffee for an added brain-boost, I got to work.

I breezed through the next few hours concentrating on putting plans for the Holt's festival into motion—and doing a fantastic job of it, if I do say so myself—until my cell phone buzzed.

Detective Shuman popped into my mind. He'd been more than a little riled up last night when I'd told him about my run-in with George at Wright's Auto Works, so I expected I'd hear from him today with details about how he'd stormed the garage, confronted the guy, demanded to know why he'd treated me so badly, and avenged my honor.

Or maybe I was getting a little carried away.

Not that it mattered, I realized, when I glanced at the caller ID screen and saw that it was Liam calling. A little glow of warmth welled inside of me.

"How's your day going?" he asked, when I answered my phone.

"Busy," I said.

"Too busy to get out of the office for a bit?"

I'm never too busy to leave work.

"What did you have in mind?" I asked.

Not that it mattered.

"How about meeting me for lunch?" Liam suggested.

"Just the boost my day needs," I told him.

"There's a Cheesecake Factory across the street from your office," he said. "Is thirty minutes enough time for you to wrap up what you're working on, and meet me there?"

"No problem," I told him, and we ended the call.

Thirty minutes?

Liam really needed to get to know me better.

I grabbed my handbag and left.

This morning I'd dressed in my charcoal-gray business suit, which I'd expertly accessorized with black and a hint of red, and had selected a classic black and white Chanel bag to complete my look. Oddly enough, Liam had also selected a gray business suit with a red power tie.

I supposed that meant something, but I wasn't sure what—other than that we looked great together.

We were seated in a booth at the Cheesecake Factory waiting for our lunches to be served. He'd asked how my day had gone so far. He was really good about that sort of thing.

I'd hit the high points, sharing with him the things that made me look good—really, there was no need for him to know absolutely everything about me just yet—then I asked him the same question.

"The usual," he told me, then shifted uncomfortably and started fiddling with his silverware.

I got a weird feeling.

"Is something wrong?" I asked.

"No—yes. Yes." He cleared his throat and sat up a little straighter. "I think I might have overstepped when I asked you to go away with me weekend after next."

My weird feeling got weirder.

Oh my God. Was he backing out? Was I sitting here in my totally fabulous outfit, planning *not* to order cheesecake for dessert so I wouldn't look like a pig at a trough in front of him, and he'd changed his mind about us taking our relationship up another notch?

I should have been angry but, really, I was sad.

"I sprang the invitation on you without any warning. I shouldn't have done that," Liam said, looking troubled. "And I should have asked if you wanted to go to the mountains, if you even liked the mountains, instead of making those decisions without consulting you."

He was upset because he thought he hadn't been considerate enough?

Liam was a keeper, all right.

"Everything's good. I'm always up for a surprise," I told him. "And if I really hadn't wanted to go to the mountains, I would have said so."

I'm not good at holding back.

He'd learn that soon enough.

Liam looked relieved. "You like to ski? Snowboard?"

"Sure," I said, then gave him a little grin I only shared with official boyfriends. "But, honestly, I'm much better at indoor sports."

"Oh, good, then—"

He froze and a few seconds passed before he realized what I was hinting at. Then I got a smile from him I'd never seen before.

"Could we move up our timetable?" he asked. "Maybe leave right now?"

Wow, this was really nice, having a special moment with Liam. He was great in so many ways, and I knew—

Oh my God, a Mystique clutch just passed by our booth.

I sprang out of my seat.

"Haley?" Liam said.

"I'll be right back," I told him, and hurried after the Mystique and the woman who was carrying it.

"Are you okay?" he called.

I didn't have time to explain. I was on a mission.

Liam would just have to learn to deal with it.

I wound my way between the tables, the servers, and their trays of food, determined to keep her in sight. Honestly, I'd had it with waiting for Nuovo to locate their missing shipment. I wanted a Mystique and I was going to get one, even if I had to give up on my stunning eighty-percent employee discount.

I followed her toward the rear of the restaurant, figuring she was headed for the restroom. I intended to ask where she'd gotten her Mystique. Obviously, one of the shops, stores, or boutiques in Los Angeles had received a shipment. I needed to find out which one it was so I could go there myself.

When we reached the ladies' room, a group of older women pushed in ahead of me. There was already a line so we all squeezed in along the wall to wait. The place was noisy, with all the chatter, the running water, and the hand dryers. I didn't really want to shout over all the racket—it's hard to sound casual under those circumstances—but no way was I going to let that

Mystique out of my sight before I found out where it had come from.

Just as I was about to make my move, I realized something wasn't quite right.

The girl carrying the handbag of my dreams looked familiar. She was probably about my age, tall, with dark hair. I definitely knew her from somewhere, but where?

My mind spun as the line for the stalls moved forward and I mentally placed her image in a variety of locations I'd been to lately, to see where it fit. A restaurant? L.A. Affairs? Holt's—no, definitely not Holt's.

Then it hit me.

She was Chandra, my personal shopper at Nuovo.

No wonder I didn't recognize her. She was dressed in a YSL pencil skirt and jacket, and she had on Louboutin pumps—mega-expensive designer wear.

Wow, Nuovo must pay better than I'd thought.

I realized then that something else was amiss.

Chandra had told me that Nuovo was waiting to receive their very first order of Mystiques. I'd also been told by Kendal that the shipment was lost.

Yet here Chandra stood with the most fabulous clutch of the moment—which, really, should have been mine—in her possession.

Huh. Interesting.

And definitely something I intended to follow up on.

Chapter 19

I was pulling double duty this afternoon, working at Holt's while I continued the planning of the festival. After lunch with Liam, I headed home, changed into jeans and an I-hope-nobody-who-matters-sees-me-in-this knit top, and drove to Holt's.

Elise, my contact in the marketing department at the Holt's corporate office, had given me the basics of what they wanted, a red, white, and blue Americana theme. The marketing wizards thought it would project a positive image of the shopping center and play well in the media. I agreed.

I'd already hired two bands to play during the event, along with four dance troupes. Holt's would stage fashion shows featuring their own yes-I-have-to-call-them-fashions clothing line. There would be a kids' area, of course, with games, face painting, and pony rides. I was also bringing in stilt-walkers, jugglers, and clowns. And all of that was just for starters.

The other businesses in the shopping center were running special sales and discounts. Jeanette had given me a preliminary list of who was doing what. I needed to check with each of them and find out exactly what they were planning. This was no time for last-minute surprises.

I stowed my handbag—an amazing Burberry satchel—but hung on to the Coach tote that held the tools of my event-planning trade as I clocked in. On the work schedule above the time clock, I saw that I was assigned to the lingerie department this afternoon. They would have to get along without me for a while.

As I left the breakroom I decided to stop by Jeanette's office and let her know everything I'd accomplished. More than likely, Elise in marketing was keeping her up to speed on the preparations, but no way was I leaving that to chance.

When I walked down the hall and stopped in her office doorway, I saw that Jeanette was at her desk, talking on the phone. She spotted me and whispered, "I'm on with corporate."

I gave her an I-understand nod, and went back into the breakroom. I mean, really, there was no reason for me to report to lingerie and do actual work for Holt's when I could be powering up with a bag or two of M&M's to get me through the afternoon's festival planning.

I hit the vending machine, then settled into a chair at one of the tables and pulled out my iPad. There were a number of things that needed my attention that I could mark off my long-and-getting-longer list of things to do.

Then it hit me—since I was on company time, why not take care of some personal business?

This thing with my mom and the Miss California Cupid beauty contest really had to be resolved. Apparently, from the way she'd explained it, the issue of the conflict of interest with one of the pageant judges had blown up the Internet, so I figured I could track it down and get it handled easily enough.

To fortify myself, I dumped half a bag of M&M's into my mouth, got out my cell phone, and did a Google search.

Three links appeared.

Not exactly the hot-button issue Mom had made it out to be.

I clicked on the links and skimmed the posts. They were mostly tirades about how demeaning beauty pageants were, how women's bodies were being exploited, and that the contests were a relic of the past that should be shelved for good.

The pro-pageant bloggers had their say, too, commenting that the contests showcased the very highest standards in young women, and offered scholarships and opportunities most of the contestants wouldn't otherwise have. Mention was made about how beauty pageants had propelled finalists on to important, high-profile careers in many industries.

Just as everything was about to turn into blah-blah-blah, another post jumped out at me, this one written by Crown Girl, that addressed the supposed conflict of interest. I clicked on the link and read the blog. It stated that Theodore Tremaine, a judge in the Miss California Cupid pageant, had slept with one of the contestants.

I couldn't help it. My mouth fell open.

This wasn't simply a conflict of interest. This was a major scandal.

I went back and read Crown Girl's blog more carefully, then dug deeper and found links to more posts. Everybody—absolutely everybody—was totally outraged that the integrity of the beauty pageant had been compromised in this manner. And, of course, speculation and accusations ran rampant about the judging of other pageants, both past and future.

Crown Girl hadn't mentioned the contestant's name. I didn't know why she'd held back, after dropping this huge bombshell, except that maybe she was trying to build momentum for some big reveal in the future. Perhaps there was money to be made, a book or movie deal, or something.

It was hard to know what motivated Crown Girl and people like her. Maybe it was a sense of justice, wanting to right a wrong. Or perhaps she was a disgruntled contestant herself who'd had no success and wanted to ruin it for everybody else. Maybe, like Asha, she was just in it for the money.

Anyway, I didn't need a degree in investigative journalism to figure out that the as-yet-unnamed guilty party was the winner of the pageant. It couldn't be more obvious. Nor was Theodore

Tremaine's conquest a secret to anyone who'd been involved in the Miss California Cupid pageant that year. Everybody knew who had finished in first place.

Mom must have been furious when this story had broken and she'd learned that another contestant had slept her way into the first-place win, leaving Mom in second.

I would be.

I wondered if Mom had known what was going on between Theodore Tremaine and whoever-she-was back in the day when the pageant was in progress. Maybe she and Mom had been friends. Maybe they were still friends. The pageant queens were a tight group.

It was possible, too, that Mom believed the whole thing was a lie, a story contrived in an attempt to undermine pageants and build a case for discontinuing them. That would explain her burning desire to distance herself from the scandal. Mom would rather downplay the incident and throw her support behind keeping beauty pageants alive.

Mom was a queen who'd never abdicate her throne.

I found a few more links, but everything was a rehash of all the other posts. One glaring omission from everything that had been written was a comment from Theodore Tremaine. Nobody had contacted him, it seemed. No one from the pageant board of directors had been asked to chime in on the scandal either, apparently.

So much for balanced reporting.

I finished off my M&M's. The sugar rush

zinged through my brain, igniting an array of cells that presented me with the idea that maybe Mom was right—which was weird, I know—and the whole incident was better left alone. Too much energy given to this sort of thing just kept it going, caused it to grow and turn into more than it likely would have been if left to wither away unattended.

But if Mom really wanted to let the whole scandal simply go away, why was she suddenly thinking about moving to Sri Lanka?

I was definitely going to investigate further.

Just as I was tucking away my cell phone, off to my right loomed what in my childhood nightmares had been a giant, green Godzilla. As I was about to dive for the floor and pull my pink, pulsating, laser sword—my weapon of choice in those nightmares—I realized that it was Jeanette.

She stood in the doorway wearing a green skirt and jacket, which she'd accessorized with yet more green.

Let me simply say it wasn't working for her.

"I just spoke with Elise at corporate," she said. "Everyone there is very concerned about the success of the festival."

"Really?" I said. "I spoke with Elise just a few hours ago and she seemed fine to me."

Which was true. I guess. Really, I hadn't paid that much attention.

The stress level of Elise, or anyone else at the corporate office, wasn't something I could play into. I had to stay focused on preparations, schedules, and handling problems that arose, not babysitting the marketing department.

Besides, I'd staged massive high-profile events for L.A. Affairs involving celebrities, A-list stars, and major power players, in world-renowned venues with hundreds of guests. I was confident I could entertain the shopping center's customers in the Holt's parking lot.

"Everything has to go smoothly when the investigative journalists are here," Jeanette said.

"I know you're concerned about the media," I told her.

"Flawlessly."

"Yes, I understand."

"No problems," Jeanette said. "None at all."

I was one annoying comment away from losing it. I mean, really, everything was in good shape at this point. Anything that might go wrong in the future would be handled. What more could I say?

"I'm heading to the other shops to confirm with the owners exactly what they're doing for the festival," I said, rising from my chair.

"Security," Jeanette said. "Elise wanted to make sure you arranged for security at the festival."

I hadn't gotten to that yet, but it was on my list.

I saw no need to mention that to Jeanette.

"But their presence can't be too obvious," she told me. "We don't want the customers—and certainly not those journalists—to know we have security forces on scene."

"I have just the firm to handle it," I told her.

I had Jack in mind, of course. And it wasn't a

conflict of interest. I'd have hired him even if we hadn't had hot, sweaty jungle sex.

Before Jeanette could come up with more questions or concerns, I slipped around her and out of the breakroom.

As I crossed the sales floor, I pulled out my cell phone and called Elise in the marketing department. Rita spotted me and gave me major stink-eye. I gave it right back to her and kept walking.

Elise picked up as I left the store.

"I just wanted you to know that everything is on schedule for the festival," I told her. "I have it handled. There are no problems, as of this minute."

"Thanks, Haley." She sighed. "The head of marketing is losing her mind over this thing. It's so last minute, and so much is riding on it."

I'd never met Elise, but she sounded young, maybe my age. I figured she was getting a lot of pressure from above in typical corporate fashion.

"I understand," I said. "But you don't have anything to worry about."

"If something comes up, you'll tell me?"

"If something comes up, I'll handle it," I said.

She sighed again. "That's good to hear. Let me know if you need anything from our end. We're all leaning forward to make this happen."

"I will," I said.

"Really, anything at all."

I stopped outside Cakes By Carrie. The enticing aroma of vanilla drifted out, zapping my thoughts in a different direction.

"Maybe you could check on something for me," I said. "I requested a handbag from Nuovo in Valencia, but they told me their shipment was lost."

Elise huffed. "That figures. Everybody here at corporate is talking about Nuovo. That chain has been nothing but problems since Holt's acquired it."

Jeez, this didn't exactly inspire my confidence.

"It's the Mystique clutch," I said. "Could you check and see when their next shipment is going to arrive?"

"Glad to," Elise said.

I thanked her and we ended the call.

As I tucked my cell phone away, my gaze crossed with that of a young woman approaching the Holt's entrance. She was attractive, a little older than me, probably, tall with dark hair. Something about her looked very familiar.

"Haley," she called and walked over.

I had no idea who she was.

"You don't remember me," she said, stopping in front of me.

I got a weird feeling.

"I'm Gwen," she said. "Gwen Bishop."

My weird feeling got weirder.

"From the other night," she said. "At Jack's condo."

My thoughts scattered.

She was related to Jack? How? Who was she?

Oh my God—was she his wife? I'd never asked if he was married—I'd never even asked if he had a serious girlfriend or was in a committed relationship.

"I have something for you," Gwen said and reached into her handbag.

What was she reaching for? A gun? Was she one of those crazed, lunatic wives? Was she going to kill me right here on this spot?

No way was I dying in the Holt's shopping center. If it took my last—literally—my last breath, I would crawl to Neiman Marcus or Nordstrom and—

"I found your credit card." Gwen held out a small plastic bag with my Visa, a comb, and lip balm sealed inside.

I felt light-headed. What was going on?

"They must have fallen out of your handbag. I found them under the hall table," she said. "I know you probably already cancelled the card, but I was afraid you'd worry about where you'd left it. That kind of thing bugs me, too."

"So you're Jack's . . ."

"Sister." She smiled.

Jack had a sister? I don't know why it surprised me, but it did—though I suppose even smoking-hot private detectives have families.

"You don't remember me, do you?" Gwen said.

"Well, no," I admitted.

"You'd been partying pretty good that night," she agreed. "I wish you hadn't left so soon. I was at Starbucks. Jack told me it was your favorite. He made me promise I'd get it for you."

Okay, I was totally confused.

"If you were at Starbucks, where was Jack?" I asked.

"Beats me," she said and rolled her eyes. "He called me at midnight and asked me to come to his condo. He carried you upstairs, then took off."

Jack wasn't there.

"He's so busy, I don't see him often," Gwen said.

We hadn't had hot, sweaty jungle sex—or any other kind.

"This is the first time he's called me to look after someone at his place."

He'd lied to me. He'd played me.

"You must be pretty special to him," Gwen said.

Jack was about to find out just how *special* I could be.

Chapter 20

After Gwen left, I walked the length of the shopping center to pull myself together, then called Jack after I calmed down. I didn't want to yell at him over the phone.

I would do that in person.

His voicemail picked up so I left a message asking him to meet me at the Holt's store to discuss providing security for the festival.

He'd likely need a security team for himself when I got finished with him.

I still had work to do and needed to confirm exactly what each of the businesses was providing by way of special promotions during the festival, so I started at the convenience store at the far end of the shopping center. Raine was on duty again. She had no idea—and even less interest—what Owen was doing sales- and discount-wise. According to Jeanette and Elise, he'd committed to offering select snacks at a sizeable discount. I made a note to contact him later and confirm his plan.

I hit the furniture store—they were raffling off area rugs—and the mail center—which was discounting all their shipping supplies—and verified that's exactly what they were offering. Next, I talked to the owner of the cigar store. He was cutting prices on all their accessories, which, between the ashtrays, lighters, cigar cases, cutters, and humidifiers, turned out to be about a zillion items—who knew?

When I walked inside Cakes By Carrie the delightful smell of baked goods gave me a pleasant sugar contact high. Carrie wasn't behind the counter, but since there were no customers in the shop, I guess she didn't have to be.

Voices drifted out from the kitchen at the rear of the store. I walked closer and spotted Carrie at a worktable, deep in conversation with Dena. I couldn't hear what was being said, but they both looked intense.

I wondered if they'd seen me approach and were talking about me.

Dena suddenly looked up. Her eyes narrowed and her expression soured, as if she thought I'd been lurking there just to eavesdrop.

I hadn't, but now I wished I had.

"Can I help you?" Carrie called, in a tone that suggested I was an inconvenience at the moment, and actually helping me was the very last thing she wanted to do.

"I need to order some cakes for the festival," I said.

Carrie and Dena exchanged a put-upon smirk and walked out of the kitchen.

"I also need to talk to you both about the special deals you're offering for the festival," I said. "I'm coordinating things for Holt's."

"I'll be next door," Dena told me, and breezed past and out of the bakery.

While Carrie fetched a clipboard with an order form on it, I fished my iPad from my tote and accessed one of my many lists.

"I have you down for discounts on a dozen cookies and on your cupcakes," I said.

"That's it," Carrie said, without looking at me. "What did you want to order?"

"I need mini-cakes for the cake walk," I told her. "Two dozen of them. Chocolate, vanilla, lemon, and spice. Buttercream icing. Decorated in red, white, and blue."

She was giving off a really bad vibe. Or maybe it was me. I did, after all, suspect her of murder.

"They'll be ready the morning of the festival," Carrie said. "Anything else?"

"No, that's it. Thanks."

She turned around and walked back into the kitchen.

Jeez, if she was this rude to all her customers, no wonder Asha wrote that terrible review about her shop.

I left and walked next door to the craft store. This was the first time I'd been there—I'm not really a crafty sort of gal—and I was surprised by the massive amount of merchandise on the shelves. There were sections for scrapbooking, knitting, and jewelry making, and large displays of baskets, artificial flowers, party supplies, and a lot of other stuff I had no idea what to do with.

Dena stood behind the counter. Seeing her up close I could tell she'd gone heavy on the makeup, trying, unsuccessfully, to disguise droops and sags, and some deep wrinkles. Her high-school blond hair looked totally fried out.

After being subjected to the two of them just now in the bakery, I doubted I'd get a better reception from her than I had from Carrie, but she surprised me.

"I know we seemed a little standoffish just now," she said, and had the good grace to look contrite. "But everybody in the center is on edge these days. First, that awful murder. Then business falls off. Now we're pinning our hopes on this festival. We have a lot at stake and a great deal to lose."

"I understand," I said because, really, I did—where the other shop owners were concerned. Dena had her dead husband's insurance money, didn't she?

"If only the police could find out who killed that girl," she said. "Have you heard if they've made any progress?"

"None that I know of."

"Really?" Dena's painted-on brows bobbed upward. "I heard you were asking around about the murder."

I figured she'd heard that from Carrie. But I'd talked to Raine at the convenience store, too.

Since Dena had brought it up, I decided to roll with it.

"Did Asha work for you here?" I asked.

The craft store wasn't on her résumé, but she could have worked here and simply not listed it. She hadn't reviewed the shop on her site. Maybe there weren't any problems or any hiccups that she could stretch out of proportion.

"Oh, no. I have my regular ladies who've worked here with me since the shop opened," Dena said. "You know, I heard that man who owns the convenience store was having an affair with that girl."

"I heard that, too."

"What do the police think? Are they checking into that wife of his?" Dena asked. "Frankly, everybody is aware that he's had a lot of affairs, and she was terribly jealous."

Dena seemed to have the inside track on all the shopping center scandals. I guess Carrie wasn't the only store owner she gossiped with.

Or maybe something else was going on. Was she trying to throw suspicion onto Owen's wife?

She must have sensed what I was thinking because she picked up a stack of flyers next to the register.

"Here are my sale items for the festival. I had these printed so I could let my customers know ahead of time," she said, and handed me one of the flyers. "BOGOs on all my baskets and art supplies, plus an additional ten percent discount on all clearance items."

"Great. Looks like you're all set," I said.

I thanked her and left the store. I couldn't shake the really weird feeling I had about her.

Of course, I'd gotten the same weird vibe from Carrie.

Maybe my I-think-she-did-it senses were out of whack.

I definitely needed a Starbucks.

With no other merchants left to talk with about the festival, I went back to Holt's—but not with the intention of doing any actual work, of course. Not in the lingerie department, which I'd been assigned to, anyway.

In the breakroom I pulled out my iPad and double-checked everything I'd done so far for the festival, then went over my list of items I had to take care of tomorrow. I still had things to follow up on, but that was normal. Every event was always a work in progress, with lot of things that required attention during all phases of the execution.

Detective Shuman flew into my head.

That sort of thing just happened to me sometimes.

I hadn't heard from him yet about his visit to Wright's Auto Works. I hoped that meant something had come of the lead I'd given him—like maybe he'd found Asha's murderer.

My cell phone chimed. I checked and saw a text message from Jack. He was here at Holt's, waiting for me at the customer service booth.

My emotions amped up.

This was just the boost my day needed.

I crammed my tote bag into my locker and hurried out of the breakroom. Jack stood near stockroom entrance.

"Back here," I told him as I brushed past.

He followed me through the swinging doors. I led the way through the giant shelving units, my anger building with every step I took.

I stopped, grabbed a bed-in-a-bag set off the shelf, gave it a roundhouse swing with everything I had, and struck him in the chest.

Jack didn't flinch. He didn't back up—he didn't even sway. And it was a king-size set.

It was really hot.

But I was still mad.

I flung the bed-in-a-bag set onto the floor and yelled, "Your sister came to see me!"

Realization dawned on Jack's face. He knew he'd been busted.

That didn't calm me, either.

"She told me the truth!"

He did a total back-down.

"Okay, look. I took you to my place and called my sister to come over. I didn't take you to your apartment because I didn't think you'd want your neighbors to see you being carried in, passed out drunk, and I got a buddy of mine to get your car so you'd have it—"

"You let me think something had really gone on between us!"

"And you believed it!"

Now Jack was mad at me—because I was mad at him. It was a total girl-move, but really hot when he did it.

"Do you think I'd take advantage of you like that?" he demanded. "After I've waited? After I backed off and respected your relationship with Ty Cameron—who never deserved you, by the way. Do you really think I'd make a move when you were passed out drunk? *That's* not the way I intend to get you into bed."

The heat between us amped up. If things got any hotter, we might set off the sprinkler system.

But now was not the time. And the Holt's stockroom was definitely not the place.

I calmed down a little and said, "You were way out of line the other day."

"You mean when I did this?" Jack moved forward and reached for me.

I shoved my palm against his chest.

Wow, his chest was really hard.

"Now you're just being a jerk," I told him.

He was quiet for a few seconds, then said, "You're right. I am. I'm sorry. The other day I thought it would be funny, you know, to tease you, to pull a prank and do that, but . . ."

"But what?"

Jack hesitated again. For a moment he looked as if he wanted to say something, something that had been festering for a while, but he just shook his head.

"But it wasn't funny," he told me. "I shouldn't have done it. I'm sorry."

The heat and anger between us dissipated while we stood there looking at each other. Finally, Jack backed up a few steps.

"Do you forgive me?" he asked.

"No."

"Then I can't work for you."

"What? You have to work for me. I need you."

"Then forgive me."

"Then say you're sorry."

"I already did. Twice."

"So would it kill you to say it again?" I demanded.

Jack hesitated then said, "Our relationship has suddenly taken a middle school turn."

"Just say it."

"Okay, I'm sorry. Again."

I huffed for another minute just to prove a point—although right now I wasn't sure exactly what it was—and said, "Fine. I accept your apology."

"Say it again."

I grinned. I couldn't help it.

He grinned back. It was *that kind* of grin.

"I'm finished with Ty," I said. "But I'm dating Liam. I'm going away with him weekend after next."

"Then go away with me *this* weekend."

Jack's grin vanished. So did mine.

"I just told you I'm dating Liam now."

"And you're sure that's what you want?"

Oh my God, he was so handsome, so hot, so *everything*, I had to force myself to say, "You know how I am about dating. This shouldn't come as a surprise to you."

Jack nodded slowly, then said, "Okay."

Another long, smoldering moment dragged by. Then Jack said, "Let me know the details of the security work you need done."

He didn't wait for an answer, just walked away. At the end of the shelving unit, he stopped.

"Oh, and by the way, women do thank me," he said.

"For not carrying them into their apartments passed out drunk?"

"Yes." Jack gave me a hot grin. "And other things."

He left the stockroom.

I collapsed onto the bed-in-a-bag set.

Chapter 21

It was a Gucci day. Definitely a Gucci day. And it was also a day that I had a lot of work to do.

I sat in my office at L.A. Affairs looking truly hot, I thought, in yet another black business suit—can you have too many black business suits?—that I'd accessorized with white and subtle touches of navy blue, all of which perfectly complemented my Gucci bag. The cool thing about working here was that no matter how dreadful you might feel or how awful the day was shaping up, everybody wore fantastic fashions and accessories, and always looked great.

I realize that sounds sort of shallow, but oh well.

After spending most of the morning locking down the timetable for the Holt's festival prep on Friday, I moved ahead with working on the other events I was tasked with staging. I made calls and sent emails, as needed, all in a timely, professional manner that would one day result in my being named Event Planner Extraordinaire of the Universe—if such a title ever existed.

Maybe I should invent it.

Anyway, since I'd spent so many hours doing actual work, I decided it was an excellent time to take a break and tend to some personal business.

Since I'd learned that the Miss California Cupid contest "conflict of interest" was really a massive pageant-world-shattering scandal, I knew the whole mess wouldn't likely go away on its own—which meant my mom would be a mess until the incident somehow disappeared. Since I didn't really want to spend my Christmas holiday in Sri Lanka, somehow I had to make that happen.

I accessed the Internet on my cell phone and did a search for Theodore Tremaine, the pageant judge involved with the scandal. A number of links appeared, stories about his community involvement in Pasadena, his duties on the boards of several charities, his dedication to the arts, his commitment to helping the underprivileged.

I found photos of him at various events, spanning what looked like four decades, taking him from a young, handsome man in his thirties, to an older, still handsome man in his seventies. In the photographs, he wore a suit or a tuxedo, depending on the occasion, and posed with other civic leaders. He looked strong and dependable, and projected the aura of a no-nonsense, levelheaded man who could be counted on to do the right thing.

Definitely not the sort of man you'd think would soil his otherwise sterling reputation by slutting it up with a beauty pageant contestant and then use his influence to award her a first-place win.

I clicked on more links and found a story detailing his fortieth wedding celebration with accompanying photos of him and his still-attractive, white-haired wife, posing alongside their three grown children and four grandchildren, and detailing their many accomplishments. Everybody looked happy and successful.

Of course, it wasn't outside the realm of possibility that Theodore—Ted, as he was referred to in the stories—had had some sort of midlife crisis back in the day. Judging from the dates of the stories, I figured he must have been in his early forties at the time he was making whoopee with the soon-to-be-crowned winner of the Miss California Cupid pageant.

Not exactly the first old guy to have a fling with a younger woman.

Regardless of Ted Tremaine's true nature, I had to find out where Crown Girl had gotten wind of this story. Hopefully, the whole thing was an exaggeration, a false memory—I mean, jeez, the guy was closing in on eighty now—or an outright lie put forth by Crown Girl to further her own agenda, whatever that might be.

The easiest way to run this story to ground was to confront Ted face-to-face. It was a long shot—but it was also the easiest way to find out the truth. Maybe he'd talk to me about it. Maybe he wouldn't. It was worth a try.

I spent a few minutes link-hopping until I found his home address, then grabbed my things and left the office.

I found the home of Ted Tremaine easily enough in an older, settled section of Pasadena. The neighborhood was quiet when I parked my Honda at the curb and got out. Down the block, a stoop-shouldered woman shuffled along while a feisty little Pomeranian tugged at the leash. Two young moms pushed strollers in the opposite direction.

The lawn and shrubs looked well-tended as I went up the walk and onto the front porch. It looked freshly painted. Somebody had decorated with pots of colorful flowers, some comfy-looking chairs, and mosaic-topped tables.

I rang the bell. A minute later I heard footsteps inside and the door opened. A young woman about my age looked out.

Not what I expected.

She had on khaki pants, a red sweater, and flats. Her hair was in a messy ponytail.

"Hi," she said, and gave me a tentative smile.

I returned her smile, introduced myself, and said, "I'm looking for Ted Tremaine."

"Oh." Her smile disappeared. "Sorry. They don't live here anymore."

I wasn't sure exactly who *they* were, but I rolled with it.

"But you know Mr. and Mrs. Tremaine?" I asked.

"Sure." She glanced back inside the house for a second, then turned to me again. "We're renting the house from them. Well, technically from their kids, I guess. They were all out here from New York, I think it was, for the funeral."

Oh, crap.

"The funeral?"

She hesitated, looking a little uncomfortable now. I needed her to keep talking, so what could I do but tell a whopper of a lie?

"I went to school with one of their granddaughters. Emily. Do you know her?" I asked, but no way was I giving her time to answer, especially since my only knowledge of the Tremaines' granddaughter was what I'd read on the Internet. "We used to come here to visit her grandparents from time to time. They were such nice people. I've been feeling kind of nostalgic lately so I thought I'd just stop by and say hello, but you're saying one of them passed away?"

"Yeah, sorry," she said. "Mrs. Tremaine. About, huh, I guess it was back last fall, maybe the end of the summer."

I managed to look suitably saddened and said, "Please don't tell me Mr. Tremaine has passed, too."

"Nursing home," she said. "I don't know for sure, but I got the impression he'd been there for a few years."

"Do you know which one?" I asked.

"No, not really—"

A little boy with curly blond hair appeared and wrapped his arms around her leg—my cue to leave.

"Well, thanks," I said, backing away.

"Do you want me to tell them you stopped by?" she called, as she lifted the boy into her arms.

"Sure, that would be great," I said.

Jeez, what else could I say?

I waved, and headed for my car.

As I slid into the driver's seat, my cell phone buzzed. I checked the caller ID screen.

Amber. Ty's personal assistant. Why was she calling?

My thoughts scattered—but not in a good way.

Was Ty back? Was he here, right here in L.A., and had gone to work at the Holt's corporate office downtown?

Maybe that wasn't it. Maybe Amber had found out he was never coming back—ever.

Or—oh my God—what if she was calling to tell me he'd been in some horrible accident? Was he injured? Maimed? In a coma? Dead?

Or worse than dead—yes, worse than dead for *me*—was he in love with someone else and getting married?

I drew in two deep breaths, and answered my phone.

"Hey, Amber, how's it going?" I tried to sound casual, but I don't think I pulled it off.

She didn't seem to notice.

"Have you heard from Ty?"

Okay, that was weird.

"No," I said. "Why?"

Amber hesitated for a few seconds, then said, "I can't find him."

Okay, that was really weird.

"You mean he's lost?"

I flashed on him buried under an avalanche on Everest; in the wreckage of a small plane atop the Himalayas; marooned on a postage stamp–sized island in the Pacific.

"He's not answering my emails or returning my calls," Amber said. "He's been good about staying in touch the whole time he's been gone. Until the last several days. I haven't heard from him at all."

"That's not like him," I agreed.

Of course, I was remembering the old Ty—not the one who'd taken off in a red convertible Ferrari Spider on a moment's notice. He'd presumably spent the past few months reassessing his life. Who knew how he might have changed?

"I thought maybe you'd heard from him," Amber said, still sounding worried. "Maybe the two of you had worked things out and were holed up somewhere together making up for lost time."

The image exploded in my mind, but I forced it away.

"If he's making up for lost time with someone, it's not me," I said, and my heart ached a little saying the words. "He's probably got a new girlfriend and he's holed up with her."

"I doubt it," Amber said. "It's just not like him to disappear like this. I'm afraid something's happened."

We were quiet for a minute or so. Amber, like me, was probably thinking the worst.

"It's probably nothing," I said. "I'm sure he's fine."

"You're right."

"He's a grown man. He can take care of himself."

"Right again."

Amber didn't sound convinced. I couldn't blame her.

"If you hear from him, will you let me know?" she asked.

"Sure," I said. But, honestly, after all this time with no word from Ty, I was certain I'd be the last one he'd contact.

We ended the call and I drove back to the 210.

As I headed up the entrance ramp, my conversation with Amber was still banging around in my mind.

She'd mentioned Ty and immediately I'd thought the worst. I'd been in total panic mode thinking something had happened to him, that he was dying, that he was getting married—that he was lost to me forever.

What was the matter with me? Why did I keep losing my mind over him?

I'd decided to stop. And that was exactly what I was going to do. For reals, this time.

I was dating Liam now. He was a great guy. I was going away with him weekend after next. That's where I needed to focus my attention.

A mocha Frappuccino would have helped.

Since there wasn't a Starbucks located nearby,

I pushed through and filled my head with one of my favorite things—fashion.

Barely a quarter of the way through my mental inventory of the romantic-getaway clothes in my closet, my cell phone rang. I jumped, thinking it was Amber calling again.

Had she heard from Ty? Was she calling to say he was fine, no big deal, forget she'd called earlier?

Or had she heard from the police, the emergency room, the Navy SEALS with news of a horrific accident?

I glanced at the ID screen and saw that it was Elise calling.

My thoughts zoomed off in another direction—I was still, of course, thinking the worst.

Had the Holt's marketing department discovered some major problem with the festival? Some disaster I hadn't anticipated?

I'm not big on suspense, so I answered her call.

"Nothing's wrong," Elise told me.

She sounded chipper, upbeat—just the boost my day needed.

"Since I've called you so many times with problems," she said, "I thought it would be cool if we talked about something happy."

I was totally on board with happy.

"Sure," I said. "What's up?"

"How do you like your bag?" she asked. "Do you have it with you, or are you saving it for a special occasion?"

My bad-news-is-coming antennae perked up.

"I'm not following you," I said

"Your handbag. The Mystique," she said. "The Nuovo store in Valencia received their shipment yesterday afternoon."

Oh, crap.

"They called you, didn't they?" Elise asked.

She sounded slightly concerned. I was, too.

"No, I haven't heard from Chandra yet," I said.

"Oh?"

Now Elise sounded really concerned.

A few seconds passed. Then she said, "I'm sure you'll hear from them any time now. Today for sure."

I tried to be generous of spirit and thought, and told myself that Chandra was probably just busy and simply hadn't gotten to my name on the wait list yet. Or maybe she'd been out sick, or had an emergency, or something.

But, honestly, I was having a little trouble believing my own wishful thinking—especially since I'd seen her carrying a Mystique at the Cheesecake Factory the other day, dressed in the latest designer clothes.

"Thanks for letting me know," I said.

Elise paused for a few seconds, then said, "If you don't hear from Chandra, or someone else at the store today, let me know. I'll follow up on it."

"I will," I said. "Thanks again."

We ended the call.

I whipped my Honda into the fast lane, hit the gas, and headed for Nuovo.

Chapter 22

Instead of parking at the curb outside of Nuovo, I turned the corner, swung into the parking garage, took the ramp up, and pulled into an empty slot on the second level. The place was about half full, which wasn't unusual for late afternoon. Moms with school-age kids had already headed home, and working women were still slaving away at their jobs.

My first instinct was to straight-arm the door to Nuovo, march up to the counter, and demand to know just where the heck my Mystique clutch was, and why nobody had called me yesterday.

But, really, I was pretty sure I knew the answer to both of those questions.

I didn't want to think the worst of someone—in this case, Chandra—but it seemed obvious to me that she'd stolen the Mystique I'd seen her carrying the other day from the shipment of handbags, and had been shining me on with that excuse about the shipment being delayed. Added to my I'm-sure-I'm-right suspicion was Elise's comment that the store had suffered a rash of supposedly waylaid merchandise.

But as much as I wanted to, I couldn't just barge into the shop and make that sort of accusation. After all, I could be wrong—I doubted it, but it was possible—and throwing down that sort of claim was hard to come back from. No way did I want to alienate anyone in the shop and jeopardize my eighty-percent employee discount.

We've all got our priorities.

I decided to take things slow—which I really didn't like doing, usually—and dug my cell phone from my handbag as I headed down the stairs to the ground floor level. I called Nuovo. Chandra answered.

"Good afternoon, Ms. Randolph," she said. "I'm so pleased to hear from you. You were on my list for today."

I froze on the sidewalk. She'd intended to call and let me know my Mystique had arrived?

Jeez, and I'd thought sure she'd stolen the handbag meant for me.

Okay, so I was wrong.

I didn't feel so great about myself.

"I wanted to let you know that our shipment of Mystique bags hasn't arrived yet," Chandra said.

I *knew* I wasn't wrong.

Am I awesome, or what?

"You didn't receive a shipment yesterday?" I asked, just to be sure.

"I'm so sorry, but we didn't. I'll let you know the moment we get your bag, of course," Chandra said. "Unless you'd prefer to make a different selection? We have the latest styles from all the best designers in stock. I could give you an even better discount on one of those."

No way was I settling for anything less than a Mystique, nor was I falling for her oh-so-obvious attempt to throw me off and cover her tracks by steering me to a different bag.

"I might do that," I lied. "What time do you get off today?"

"I'll be here for another hour," she said. "But if you want to come in later, I'll be happy to stay. Just let me know."

"Thanks," I said, and we ended the call.

I walked to the end of the block and gazed down the street at Nuovo. I was really tempted to go inside and confront anyone and everyone who happened to be there right now.

I'm not good at holding back.

Instead, I did what anybody who suspected that a crime had been committed would have done—I headed to Macy's to do some shopping.

"What are we doing?" Detective Shuman asked.

"We're on a stakeout," I told him.

"We are?"

"Just roll with it."

Okay, so this wasn't the sort of stakeout a homicide detective was used to. I got that. But the most fabulous clutch bag in the entire history of all known civilization was involved, so what else could I do?

We were seated on a bench in a small courtyard amid a maze of upscale office buildings. To our left were the rear exits of a line of shops, and to our right was the parking garage designated for employees only.

The shop I was watching, of course, was Nuovo. Chandra had told me when her shift ended. I figured she'd leave through the store's rear door and head for her car in the parking garage.

I wasn't sure exactly what I intended to do when I saw her, but I was confident I'd know when the moment presented itself.

While I'd been shopping at Macy's, Shuman had texted me stating he had some info to share, so I'd told him to meet me here.

I mean, really, if you're going to be on a stakeout, why not do it with a trained professional—who also happened to be a hot-looking guy who was fun to hang out with?

We made a bit of a mismatched pair—me in my black business suit and Shuman in his questionable-fashion combo, a navy-blue sport coat and a yellow shirt that he'd paired, apparently for no good reason, with a turquoise necktie. Still, we were inconspicuous and semi-undercover enough not to raise eyebrows since the people coming and going around us hadn't given us a second look.

I figured Shuman's day had been easy, or as easy as a homicide detective's day can get. He seemed relaxed, but I sensed the undercurrent of caution and suspicion that seemed to always flow through him. I guess that came with the job. It was probably tough to completely let down your guard when spending your days seeing the absolute worst in people.

"Did you find anything new on Asha's murder investigation?" Shuman asked.

He'd texted me because he had info to share, but, of course, he wasn't going to be the first one to divulge anything. I wished I could accommodate him.

"Nothing," I said. "Honestly, I've been spending most of my time putting together the festival for Holt's. It's a super rush. Everybody at the corporate office and at the store is stressing out over it, wanting to make sure it goes smoothly for the investigative journalists who'll be there."

He nodded.

"It would help if Asha's murder was solved before they got here," I said. "Have you come up with anything?"

Shuman didn't answer right away.

I think he enjoyed making me wait—which I totally understood since I have some control issues on my own, or so I've been told.

Finally, he said, "I talked to George Wright at the auto repair shop."

"Did he confess?" I asked.

"Yes, but not to Asha's murder," he said. "He admitted paying what amounted to bribery to her for advertisements on her Exposer website."

I felt a spark of anger.

"He took out ads, expensive ads, to keep her from writing bad things about his business?" I asked.

"Yes, he did."

"Those must have cost him a fortune," I said. "How could they not, considering Asha's lavish lifestyle?"

"Cheaper than having his business's reputation ruined," Shuman said. "He has a family, a mortgage, a couple of kids heading for college. He couldn't afford to take the financial hit."

My opinion of Asha sunk even lower, though I hadn't thought that was possible.

"Did he know she was dead?" I asked.

Shuman nodded. "He'd heard."

"The news probably perked up his day considerably," I said, which, I know, wasn't a very nice thought, but still. "No more paying for overpriced ads he didn't want."

"Which is why he lashed out at you when you showed up at his garage," Shuman said. "He thought you were taking over the site from Asha."

Wow, I hadn't thought about that—and I didn't feel so great knowing that my presence had caused him so much grief.

"No wonder he was so upset with me," I said.

Then something else hit me.

"This makes him a suspect in Asha's murder," I said.

"He had motive," Shuman agreed. "If he got rid of Asha he wouldn't have to fork out money for those ads, and he wouldn't have to worry that she'd ruin his business with one of her reviews."

"Does he have an alibi?"

"Says he was at the garage that day," Shuman said. "He's in and out, running errands. He owns the place so nobody keeps track of him. Pinning down his exact schedule on the day of the murder would take some work."

"What about Valerie Roderick?" I asked.

"Her alibi checks out."

I was relieved to drop Valerie from my mental list of suspects.

Nuovo's rear door opened and Chandra walked out. She had on the same plain black dress all the clerks wore, and her hair was in a neat bun. A large tote bag was hooked over her shoulder.

She studied her cell phone as she hurried toward the parking garage. I studied her tote bag.

It was made of simple cotton fabric printed with yellow, blue, and orange flip-flops, and had a heavy braided cloth handle.

Definitely not a designer bag.

The sides bulged and she struggled to keep the straps from falling off of her shoulder. The bag was filled with something—my Mystique clutch, maybe?

"Wait here," I told Shuman, and got to my feet.

"Where are you going?" He sounded concerned, maybe slightly alarmed.

"Just wait here. I'll be right back."

He might have said something else, but I didn't hang around to listen. I cut across the sidewalk and intercepted Chandra just before she reached the parking garage.

"What's in the bag?" I demanded, planting myself in front of her.

She stopped short. Her head jerked up. A few what-the-heck seconds passed before she recognized me.

"Oh, Ms. Randolph, how nice to—"

"Save it for the store," I told her, and pointed to her tote bag. "Show me what's in there."

Chandra drew back and straightened her shoulders. "This is my personal stuff. You have no right to see it."

"No?" I nodded toward Shuman. "Well, he does."

She turned. Shuman was on his feet, frowning, and watching us.

"He's an LAPD detective," I said.

She rolled her eyes. "He is not. He's your boyfriend."

"Are you kidding? Look at how he's dressed," I said.

She gave Shuman the once-over and her expression darkened. "Oh. Yeah, that's bad."

"Look, Chandra, everybody knows shipments have been supposedly lost. You're stealing merchandise from the store," I said. "You've been smuggling it out in that tote bag, thinking nobody would notice because the thing is so crappy."

"I don't know what you're talking about," she told me. "I'm off work, and I don't have to listen to this."

Chandra cut around me and disappeared

into the parking garage. I let her go. What else could I do, short of starting a throw-down?

"I thought I was about to see a chick fight." Shuman appeared next to me. "What was that about?"

"A handbag."

He didn't seem surprised.

"How about a Starbucks?" he asked.

Shuman knew me well.

It was way cool.

"Come on," he said. "We'll go talk about murder. Not only is George Wright now a suspect, but so are the dozens of other business owners who advertised on Asha's website."

Oh, crap.

Chapter 23

I woke this morning with crime on my mind. Crimes that someone else had committed, not a crime I intended to commit—so far, anyway; the day wasn't over. I was working my afternoon shift at Holt's. Anything could happen.

"I need to get on camera," Bella told me as we pulled T-shirts off a display stand in the misses department and stacked them onto a U-boat. "You know, when those investigative journalists get here. I need to be seen."

"You want to be interviewed about the murder?" I asked.

Her expression soured. "No, that whole dead-girl thing is b.s. if you ask me. Television is full of long, in-depth stories about murders of people nobody ever heard of. Just a way to fill airtime."

I couldn't disagree.

"So why do you want to get on camera?" I asked.

"The world needs to see my hairstyles." Bella pointed to what looked like a 3D gift box complete with a huge bow that she'd shaped atop her head. "Cool stuff, don't you think?"

"Your best design yet," I agreed.

"So, see? Here's my plan—I get on camera and show off my do, then everybody all across America gets a look at my unique work," Bella said, gently patting the sides and back of her head. "I'll *just happen* to let it slip that I'm saving for beauty school so I can bring my own brand of hair styles to the world and, bang, the donations start pouring in."

"You think so?"

"Damn straight." She gestured to her hair again. "Who would see this and not be struck speechless?"

She had me there.

"Hey, guys," Sandy called.

She rolled up to the display stand pushing a U-boat loaded with stacks of new merchandise. I couldn't tell exactly what it was. More T-shirts, maybe. All I knew for sure was that these bedazzled floral prints embellished with tiny bows and hearts weren't likely to make the cover of *Vogue*.

"Tonight's the big night," Sandy announced, as she grabbed a stack of outgoing T-shirts off of the display stand.

"Oh, yeah, your birthday dinner with your boyfriend," Bella said. "Is that still on? He hasn't backed out, has he?"

"Of course not," she said, bouncing on her toes and smiling. "I am so super excited."

I felt kind of bad that I hadn't gotten Sandy anything for her big day, but my Holt's BFFs didn't exchange presents. Really, most everybody who worked here was struggling to make ends meet. Exchanging gifts was a tradition nobody could really afford.

"Happy birthday," I said.

"Actually, my birthday is tomorrow," she said.

"So why is your boyfriend taking you out to celebrate tonight instead of tomorrow?" Bella asked.

"He can't do it tomorrow," Sandy said. "He's got a family reunion that he has to go to."

"You're not going to the family reunion with him? How come?" Bella asked. "You two have been dating for, what, more than a year now? And you haven't met his family yet?"

"He's an artist," Sandy explained. "He has to feel something is truly right before he moves on it."

Bella and I exchange a yeah-right eye roll.

I grabbed the last stack of T-shirts from the display and dropped them onto the U-boat.

"Have a good time tonight," I said.

"Oh, I will," Sandy said.

I headed down the aisle, pushing the U-boat ahead of me. I didn't have a good feeling about Sandy's big birthday night out with her boyfriend, but maybe it was just me. After all, I woke up this morning with Asha's murder investigation weighing heavily on my mind.

After learning from Shuman yesterday that

George Wright at the auto repair place had a reason to want Asha dead—which meant that everyone else who advertised on her site wanted pretty much the same thing—I didn't see how Asha's murder could be solved before the investigative reporters arrived. No way could Shuman, even with the massive resources available at the LAPD, work his way through that long list of names, check out each and every one of them, and establish an alibi—or not.

Faced with those odds, there was nothing I'd like more than to solve this case myself. It would be totally cool. Shuman would be so impressed. I felt sure I could do it. I just needed one key piece of evidence or information that would bring everything together.

All I had to do was find it.

As I turned the corner near the housewares department, I spotted Jeanette in menswear, chatting with that big guy who works there.

Yikes! No way did I want to get stuck talking with her. I knew she'd want to ask me a zillion questions about the festival and, really, there was nothing new I could tell her.

I'd spent the morning at L.A. Affairs confirming—and re-confirming—that everything was in place for the festival. Preparation would begin tomorrow morning, on schedule, as promised. Likewise, every last detail was ready to go for the festival's kickoff on Saturday.

I wouldn't be here now, I wouldn't have left L.A. Affairs this morning, if anything else needed to be handled.

Before Jeanette could spot me, I whipped the U-boat around and headed the other way.

At the entrance to the stockroom, I pushed the U-boat through the swinging doors and down the aisles. This load of T-shirts was being returned to the manufacturer, for some reason. I didn't know what it was. Surely, not simply because they were hideous—if so, all our shelves would be empty.

I reached the returns area of the stockroom. The place was quiet. Nobody else was around.

Instead of off-loading the T-shirts, I decided this particular chore could wait—really, there's always a good reason to put something off. I sank onto the bottom step of the staircase that led to the second floor, thoughts of murder suspects filling my head again.

First, there was the wife of the convenience store owner. She had one of the oldest and most justified motives around—really, anyone who cheated on a spouse ought to be shot.

But why she'd gone after Asha and not that scumbag husband of hers, I didn't know. Still, it was an excellent motive, and the rear of the Holt's shopping center made a convenient place to commit the crime. Plus, she had no alibi for the time of the murder, according to Shuman.

Carrie had motive and opportunity, two really important items on my mental yeah-she-probably-did-it list. Asha had trashed her bakery on the Exposer site, and she'd been killed just steps from the rear exit to Carrie's shop.

But what about means? Shuman hadn't found

a gun registered in Carrie's name. That didn't exclude the possibility that she owned an unregistered weapon, or had somehow gotten one from somebody she knew.

Dena owned a gun—she'd used it to accidentally shoot her own husband. She had opportunity.

But what could have been her motive? Asha hadn't written a scathing review about her craft store, and I hadn't seen an ad on the Exposer site that Dena might have placed there to keep Asha happy, as George at Wright Auto Works—and probably others—had done.

Of course, there were dozens of other potential suspects that Shuman was sorting through. Maybe the killer was someone I hadn't even met.

Still, I couldn't help but feel that something major was missing. Some piece of the puzzle that hadn't been discovered yet. A connection of some sort that hadn't been made, which, once revealed, would tie everything together.

Maybe it was the proximity of the shops in the center to the crime scene. Was it simply a coincidence? I doubted it. More likely, the killer had seen Asha here, making this a crime of opportunity. Or followed her there. Did somebody want her death tied to Holt's?

I was getting nowhere, and my brain was starting to hurt.

I desperately needed a mocha Frappuccino.

Just as I was contemplating coming up with a good excuse to leave Holt's early today, another crime popped into my head.

Chandra and my Mystique clutch.

I looked around at the shelves teeming with fresh, new merchandise, every possible item for every member of the family, all just sitting there. How easy it would be for an employee to slip back here, put a few things in a handbag or pocket, and smuggle them out of the store. Times were hard for a lot of people, including the Holt's employees, and it was surely tempting to walk off with a pack of socks or underwear, or something more expensive.

It must have been really tempting for Chandra, working in a store that carried designer fashions that she could keep for herself, or easily sell to her friends or online for a ton of cash.

There was little in place to prevent an employee from stealing a store's merchandise—the honor system, a personal code of conduct, and, of course, the fear of getting caught and losing your job. Those things deterred most workers but surely not everyone.

I considered calling the Holt's corporate office and ratting out Chandra. But, honestly, it was doubtful they would do anything. I had no real proof. And even if I did, theft was tough to prove unless the employee was caught redhanded. Plus, that sort of crime was hardly worth the legal fees and expenses necessary to prosecute the suspected culprit.

Maybe I'd frightened Chandra enough with my accusation that she'd suddenly come up with Mystique clutches for Marcie and me to keep me quiet. Or maybe she'd quit and her replacement would see to it we got our bags.

Otherwise, I didn't know how I was going to get my hands on that Mystique.

Not a great feeling.

My day definitely needed a boost.

I'd had enough thoughts of murder for one day. I needed to move to a problem I could definitely find a conclusion to—the beauty pageant scandal.

I stacked the T-shirts onto the returns counter, parked the U-boat, and hurried to the breakroom. After I dashed off a quick email to Jeanette stating something had come up with the festival that needed my immediate attention—a big fat lie, but oh well—I clocked out and left the store.

I drove to Starbucks, and while I sat in the drive-through line, I Googled nursing homes in Pasadena on my cell phone. The young mom whom I'd met at Ted Tremaine's old family home had mentioned that he'd been placed in a care facility several years ago. His wife had still been alive at that time, so I figured she would have selected a place close to their house so she could visit easily and often.

As the line moved forward, my Google search presented me with over a dozen nursing homes.

Jeez, how many old sick people were in Pasadena?

I picked the one closest to the Tremaine home, punched the address into my GPS, got my mocha Frappuccino, and took off.

Four nursing homes, one mocha Frappuccino, and numerous maybe-I-should-find-a-different-search-method thoughts later, I rolled up to the Golden Years Care Center just off of Fair Oaks Avenue. It was a one-story building surrounded by trimmed shrubbery, colorful flowerbeds, and towering trees that were probably younger than most of the residents.

I parked and went inside. The lobby had tile floors, serviceable furniture, and halfway decent wall art, all in pleasant, neutral tones. Two middle-aged couples were crowded together on a sofa, murmuring and looking tense, probably waiting for a tour that would decide the fate of a parent.

Behind the long, high reception counter stood a forty-something woman with sensible dark hair, wearing an it-was-on-the-clearance-rack-so-I-bought-it pale blue dress. I walked up and waited while she shuffled some papers around before she acknowledged my presence.

"Hi," I said, giving her my you-can-trust-me-smile. "I'm here to visit one of your residents. Theodore Tremaine."

I was ready with my oh-no-you're-kidding story that I'd perfected at the previous four care facilities I'd visited when I'd been told no one by that name lived there. So I was surprised when the woman pulled out a binder, opened it to a page with Theodore Tremaine's name at the top, and placed it on the counter in front of me.

"Sign in, please," she said. "And I'll need to see your ID."

I guess that was it for security, but, really, what else did they need? Nobody was boarding an aircraft here or visiting a prisoner.

After I signed in and watched as she wrote down my info, she handed back my driver's license and closed the logbook with a snap.

"Ted is in one-twelve. But he's probably in the day room. That's where he usually spends his time." She pointed. "Through the double doors, turn left, and you'll see it at the end of the corridor. Enjoy your visit, Ms. Randolph."

I thanked her and headed for the day room.

The double doors opened into a long corridor. The place smelled of pine cleaner. The floors sparkled. Everything looked neat and orderly. Caregivers dressed in pastel uniforms bustled through the corridor looking pleasant and competent. The residents moved along at a much slower pace, some of them on walkers, others in wheelchairs.

The day room at the end of the corridor was a large space filled with numerous seating groups, two televisions, a bookcase of paperbacks, and a table with a half-completed jigsaw puzzle. Large windows let in natural light and offered a view of the rear of the property, a garden setting with wide walking paths, benches, a fountain, and lots of shade trees.

A dozen or so residents were scattered throughout the room, some sitting together while a few others were seated alone. Nobody looked up when I walked in.

I hoped that meant the folks confined to this place routinely got visitors, so spotting a stranger was no big deal.

I'd figured that after seeing so many photos of Ted online, I would recognize him. Now I wasn't so sure. In the pictures, he'd looked strong and healthy, even in the recent shots of him with his mane of white hair.

No one here looked like that.

A caregiver wearing a blue uniform and comfy shoes paused beside me on her way out of the day room. She must have realized my predicament because she said, "Looking for someone?"

"Ted Tremaine," I said.

I was ready to let loose with my I'm-a-friend-of-his-granddaughter story, but she didn't give me a chance.

"Over there. In the wheelchair." She pointed across the room, to the window, then kept walking.

Ted seemed like a smaller version of his former self. His white hair had thinned considerably. His face, neck, and arms looked boney, as if he'd somehow shrunk, making the khaki pants and checked shirt he wore seem several sizes too big.

"Hello, Ted," I said, stopping next to his wheelchair.

He looked up, his brilliant blue eyes locking onto my face. I hadn't been sure what sort of reception I'd get, a complete stranger showing up out of nowhere, but he smiled, displaying the flash of youth and vitality I'd seen in those online photos.

"Well, hello there."

I grabbed a chair from the jigsaw puzzle table, pulled it over, and sat down beside his wheelchair, facing him.

"I wonder if it would be all right if I talked to

you about a beauty pageant you judged," I said. "It was the Miss California Cupid contest. You might remember, it was about—"

He gasped. One hand shot to his chest, the other reached out to me.

I went immediately into semi-panic mode. What was happening? Was he having a heart attack?

I was about to jump up and go for help when he grabbed my hand. His fingers felt cold and papery, but his grip was strong. He stared at me, squinting, tilting his head left, then right, finally leaning closer.

"Caroline?" he croaked.

Oh my God.

"Caroline?" A smile broke over his face. "Caroline Vander Meer? Is that really you?"

He thought I was my mom.

"You're as beautiful as ever," he said, grasping my hand with both of his. "You haven't changed a bit."

He thought I was my mom back in the day.

I didn't know what to say or do. Obviously, Ted suffered from dementia, or maybe Alzheimer's.

Yikes! No way did I want to get old.

I didn't want to be here any longer, either. Besides, in his mental state, I didn't see how he could give me any information about the Miss California Cupid scandal. All I could think to do was ride it out until I could slip away.

"Oh, Caroline," he said, his smile growing wider.

Jeez, what was I supposed to do? It didn't seem right to let him think I was my mom.

"Actually, Caroline is—"

"You were the cutest little cupid in the pageant," Ted said, giving my hand a squeeze. He sighed and closed his eyes for a second, then said, "I knew you'd come back."

Come back? What the heck was he talking about?

"A man in my position." He winked. "Anything for a pageant crown, huh, Caroline?"

Oh my God. *Oh my God.*

The scandalous rumor was true. One of the pageant contestants *had* slept with Theodore Tremaine—and it was my *mom.*

Mom had fooled around with—

Hang on a second.

Mom had sex with a pageant judge and she'd placed second? *Second?*

Oh, crap.

Chapter 24

I needed a shower.

No, wait. A shower wouldn't be enough. I needed to scrub my brain clean of the image of Mom and Ted Tremaine having hot, sweaty jungle sex—*somehow.*

Yeah, okay, I was all grown up, a mature adult, but this whole thing sent me into major, middle school gross-out mode.

Mom. Having sex—actual sex.

No child should have to face that.

I hurried from the day room, anxious to get out of the nursing home, into my car, onto the freeway, perhaps never to return to Pasadena in my entire life.

Oh my God, how was I ever going to look at my mom again without thinking about this?

I banged through the double doors, my vision laser sharp on the exit across the lobby.

Then it hit me—I hadn't solved the problem. I hadn't found a way to end the scandal. I couldn't leave.

Crap.

I stopped and drew in several breaths. I waited for my heart rate and breathing to slow to normal. A moment passed, then another.

Nothing returned to normal.

Oh my God, did that mean I was never going to get over this?

I darted to the reception desk.

"I need to speak with the director." I might have said that kind of loud.

The woman behind the counter whipped around.

"Now!" I'm sure I said that loud. Really loud.

Her eyebrows disappeared under her bangs, her eyes bugged out.

"Or there's going to be a lawsuit so huge it will bury this place!" Yeah, I screamed that.

She grabbed the telephone—hopefully she wasn't calling security—and murmured something that included my name and Ted Tremaine's, then hung up.

"The director will see you now." She pointed to the double doors. "Turn right, halfway down the corridor on your left."

I headed that way—thank goodness I didn't have to walk past the day room—and found the office. A nameplate was positioned next to the open door that read: JOSEPHINE RAMSEY, DIRECTOR.

Inside was a small seating area and a desk occupied by a receptionist, a middle-aged woman with red hair who gave off a weary don't-bother-because-I've-already-seen-it-all vibe.

"Go on in," she said, and nodded toward the connecting office.

Josephine Ramsey rose from behind her desk when I walked in. Yikes! She was tall—taller than me, easily over six feet with heels. To be generous, I'll say she looked sturdy in a Michael Kors business suit, with a helmet of jet-black hair, full-on makeup, and her nails done.

She introduced herself and pointed to the chair in front of her desk. "Tell me what's wrong, Ms. Randolph."

As soon as we sat down, I blasted her with the scandalous online story that had been posted by Crown Girl, which, really, was not the best way to handle the situation. But, come on, I was still completely rattled and she was the director—who else could I take it out on?

"This incident was meant to embarrass, humiliate, and ruin Mr. Tremaine's sterling reputation in the community," I said. "Crown Girl took advantage of his diminished mental capacity and exploited it for her own gain. She used inside knowledge that should be confidential, and abused her position of trust in this care facility."

"So this woman who calls herself Crown Girl, how do you know she works here?" Josephine asked.

Crown Girl had to be an employee. I was sure of it.

Ted Tremaine's wife was dead, his kids lived

out of state, and likely all his friends were as old as he was and not in any better health, so no way would they visit him here—and even if they had and he'd blabbed about what happened at the pageant, no way would they have posted it online.

Plus, I'd seen the sign-in log at the receptionist's desk.

"He hasn't had a visitor in three months. The story was posted online a week ago. Who else could have done it?" I said.

She didn't say anything, so I went on.

"This situation is inexcusable. It's elder abuse."

She knew without me saying it that *elder abuse* was code for *lawsuit*.

And once word got out that Golden Years Care Center was embroiled in legal trouble stemming from an employee and claims of elder abuse, the place would be out of business in no time; Pasadena wasn't exactly short on nursing homes.

Josephine drew herself up and a look of determination came over her face that was—yikes!—kind of scary.

"I will not have this facility's reputation ruined under any circumstances. I, and everyone else on staff, have worked long and hard to ensure high standards and a quality environment, and to provide the best possible care of our residents," Josephine said. "This situation will not be tolerated. I simply won't allow it. Not after all the hard work that's gone into it."

She sounded like a woman on a mission.

"Rest assured, this Crown Girl's identity will

be discovered and that post will be taken down immediately." Josephine stood up and leaned toward the receptionist in the adjoining office. "Helen! Get legal on the phone. I want HR in my office immediately. And call a staff meeting."

I figured my work there was done. I rose from my chair.

"My door is always open," Josephine said. "If there are other problems, please come to me."

It was nice of her to say that, but, really, no way was I ever coming back here again.

"Thank you," I said.

I left the care facility totally exhausted and still partially grossed out. There was nothing to do, of course, but head to Starbucks.

I drove to the closest one, which, luckily, was only a few blocks away. Instead of going through the drive-through, I went inside, got my Frappie, and found a table in the back corner. Only two other people were there, one of them on a laptop and the other reading a newspaper. I was glad for the quiet.

Honestly, I'd been impressed with Josephine Ramsey. She'd knocked it out of the park, as far as I was concerned, in her efforts to squelch Crown Girl's post and put an end to this sort of thing ever happening again. Obviously, she knew the importance of her facility's reputation. Once it was tarnished, once the public got the idea in their collective heads that there were problems at Golden Years Care Center, turning that around could be almost impossible.

Josephine wasn't playing around. She meant

business. She wasn't going down without a fight. I liked that.

Thinking about Josephine zapped my brain, sending my thoughts in a different direction, kind of.

Had Carrie felt that strongly about her bakery? Had she been so mad, so upset, so outraged by the review on the Exposer site that had crippled her business that she'd killed Asha?

Of course, several months had passed between the time of the review and the murder. If Carrie was protective enough of her bakery to kill Asha, wouldn't she have done it sooner?

Then it hit me—maybe not.

What if Asha had come to Carrie demanding she take out an advertisement on her Exposer website? What if she'd threatened to write another scathing review if she didn't?

I sat straight up in my chair. Oh my God, that was what had happened. It *had* to be.

Images and possibilities filled my head, spinning out the whole story.

Carrie was friendly with the craft store owner, Dena, who owned a gun. What if Carrie had somehow gotten it from her? What if she'd arranged a meeting with Asha under the guise of taking out an ad on her site?

Oh my God, Carrie had lured Asha to the rear of the store and shot her. It made perfect sense.

Fishing my cell phone out of my handbag, I grabbed my Frappie and hurried out of Starbucks as I punched in Shuman's number.

"I know who killed Asha," I announced when he picked up.

"Is that so?"

He didn't sound nearly as amped up as I felt. Why wasn't he shouting, cheering, maybe laying the phone aside to turn a cartwheel?

"Yes," I said, pacing back and forth on the sidewalk. "It was Carrie. The owner of the bakery."

Shuman didn't say anything.

"Asha nearly ruined her business—the thing that meant the most to her in the world," I said. "There's nothing people care more about than the reputation of their shop or store—you know that's true."

Shuman was quiet for a few seconds, then asked, "Did you come up with some evidence?"

Okay, now he was getting kind of picky, but I rolled with it.

"No—but you did," I insisted.

He didn't ask what it was.

Jeez, what was the matter with Shuman? I'd made a major breakthrough here. I'd solved the case. Why wasn't he all over this?

I slurped the last of my Frappie and said, "You talked to George, the guy who owned Wright's Auto Works, remember? Asha forced him to take out an advertisement to prevent her from ruining his business with a stinky review. That's extortion. Plain and simple."

Shuman didn't comment.

"I'll bet Asha tried to do the same thing with Carrie and her bakery," I told him. "She pressured her to take out an ad. Carrie already knew how detrimental a bad review could be, so no way could she not go along with it. She *had* to agree to buy the ad."

"We looked," Shuman said. "There was no ad on the Exposer site from Cakes By Carrie."

"Yes, but I'll bet Asha had a list of potential advertising customers somewhere in her files," I told him. "You have her laptop. Check it out. I know you'll find something. It's the connection we've been missing. I'm sure of it."

"What about a murder weapon?" he asked.

Now he was being really picky, but I was ready.

"Carrie is friends with Dena. Dena's shop is next door to the bakery. Maybe Dena keeps the gun at her craft store? She has a license to carry concealed, remember? Maybe Carrie knew about it? Maybe she sneaked in there and got it, and killed Asha?"

"I'm hearing a lot of *maybes*."

Oh my God, Shuman was totally not on board with my stunning solution to Asha's murder. What was the matter with him?

I walked to the trash can and dropped my cup in.

"Look," I said, "just think about it. It makes perfect sense. Get your computer guys to check out Asha's laptop. There's a list of advertisers there and Carrie is one of them, I just know it."

Shuman was quiet for a few seconds, then said, "Okay. I'll interview Carrie again."

Visions of SWAT rolling up to the bakery, hot guys loaded down with weapons rappelling from hovering helicopters blooming in my head.

No way did I want to miss that.

"Great," I said. "I'll meet you there in less than an hour."

"Tomorrow," Shuman said. "It will have to be tomorrow."

Crap.

"Okay, but let me know when you get there," I said.

"I will," Shuman said, and ended the call.

Huh. Not exactly the stunning "Yeah, you did it!" I'd expected—or thought I deserved—but still, I was happy.

Just to keep the good thoughts rolling, I was considering treating myself to yet another Frappuccino when my brain was slammed with the image of Mom and Ted doing the humpty-bump back in the day.

Gross.

I walked to one of the umbrella tables and dropped into a chair.

No way was I ever—ever—going to get over this.

Then something else hit me.

Mom had sex with the pageant judge—and she'd placed second. *Second.* How humiliating was that?

Then, suddenly, a bright spot flashed in this darkest moment in my life and I perked up.

Second, huh?

Did that mean I was finally better at something than my mom?

Oh, yeah.

Chapter 25

I had a lot of things to do this morning. I'd scheduled workers to arrive at Holt's super early to block off the parking lot and begin setting up for tomorrow's festival. Throughout the day, I would oversee different phases of preparation. All normal stuff.

I'd dressed in black pants and sweater, and put my hair in an I'm-in-charge-but-I'm-still-fun low ponytail, my usual event planner's uniform for prep day.

But I didn't head for Holt's when I left my apartment. The festival staging would have to proceed without me for a while. I wasn't worried. The companies I'd hired to do the work were top-notch. I'd dealt with them before. And if a problem arose, they would give me a call.

First thing this morning when I rolled out of bed, I'd checked the Internet. I was anxious to see if Josephine Ramsey had come through with her pledge of getting Crown Girl's post taken down. She had. The story was nowhere to be found.

Now I was headed to Mom's house to give her the news. I could have called her, but I felt this was something I had to do in person—and I had to be a mature adult about it, somehow.

When I exited the 210 and wound through the streets toward my parents' house, the other major situation in my life flew into my head.

All night, I'd thought about my startling revelation yesterday that Carrie had murdered Asha, and I was still convinced I was right—even though Shuman hadn't seemed excited about my solving the case for him. He'd promised to interview Carrie again today and, hope-fully, he'd uncover some crucial info that would put an end to the investigation today—or she would confess. It sure would make things easier on everybody when those investigative journalists showed up at the festival tomorrow.

When I pulled into my parents' driveway, I parked and jumped out of my Honda. Juanita opened the front door before I got there. She looked tense.

Not a good sign.

"She's in that same room," she said, wringing her hands.

"Relax," I said. "Everything's fine. The problem disappeared."

"Are you sure?" Juanita still looked troubled.

"Don't worry. Nobody's moving to Sri Lanka, or anywhere else."

I headed through the house to the media room. The lights were low; the television was off. Mom sat on the sofa. She had on jeans and a sweatshirt—which I hadn't even known she owned. Her hair was still wet from the shower, she had on no makeup, and she was staring off at nothing.

"Good news, Mom," I announced, as I walked over.

A few seconds passed before she looked up at me.

"Oh, Haley. Hi, sweetie." She looked lost for a moment. "I wasn't expecting you this morning. Or was I?"

"I came by to tell you something," I said, and dropped onto the sofa next to her. "That story about the Miss California Cupid pageant has been taken down. It's not on the Internet. It's gone for good."

Mom looked stunned, as if she didn't really comprehend what I was saying.

"You don't have to worry about anybody gossiping about the pageant or anything," I said.

"How . . . how do you know?"

She'd made me promise not to get involved so I didn't want to tell her I'd gone against her wishes. I was afraid divulging the truth about my visit to the Golden Years Care Center would upset her further.

"I read it on the Internet," I said.

It was a lie, of course, but it could have happened.

"The whole story was a complete fabrication,

apparently, written by someone who just wanted to stir up trouble. You know how those Internet things are," I said.

Mom didn't look convinced so I went on.

"And I heard there was a threat of a lawsuit," I said. "That's why the story was taken down, and why it will never be mentioned again."

She chewed her bottom lip and glanced away for a few seconds, then looked at me again.

"You're certain?"

"Absolutely."

Mom drew a breath and let it out slowly, then said, "That is good news. Thank you, sweetie, for coming over and letting me know."

I'd expected her to be happier, more relieved that the situation was over and done with, never to return. Instead, she still looked . . . sad.

"Aren't you happy, Mom?" I asked.

She gazed across the room again and said, "This incident has given me a lot of time to think and . . . remember."

I glanced back over my shoulder and saw that she was staring at the *Back to the Future* movie poster again.

Was she looking at it, wishing she could go back in time before Crown Girl posted that story and started this whole upsetting situation?

I figured that must be it. I mean, what else—

Then it hit me.

There was another reason Mom wanted to go back, maybe all the way back to the Miss California Cupid contest.

She had been nineteen at the time. Ted had been a handsome, wealthy, sophisticated older man. Her tryst with him had been something more than a fling.

She'd actually been in love with him.

Looking at her now, seeing that haunted expression on her face, I knew I was right.

Had Ted felt the same about her?

I didn't know, but I hoped he did.

Obviously, they'd ended it.

Their age difference—some twenty years—was significant. He'd been married and probably had children by then. These were major hurdles, not easily overcome.

I wondered which one of them had made the decision.

I wondered, too, if I'd been wrong about Mom's concern over Crown Girl's tell-all. This whole thing wasn't about Mom's reputation, if it came to light that she was the contestant who'd slept with a judge. Maybe she wasn't even worried so much about the public's perception of beauty pageants.

It was Ted's reputation she wanted to keep intact.

My thoughts jumped to my dad. Where did he fit into this? Had Mom *settled* for him?

Mom and Dad were an odd pair. They were total opposites, so I'd often wondered why they'd married. I'd always figured it had been true love.

Now I wasn't so sure.

"Thank you, Haley," Mom said. "Thank you for coming over here to give me the news."

"You know, Mom, if you ever want to talk about anything, I'm here for you."

She smiled the genuine mom-smile I'd seen all my life.

"And I'm here for you." She paused for a moment. "I know things are often strained between us. We're so different. But there's nothing I wouldn't do for you."

"I know, Mom," I said.

"No, you don't." She shook her head. "You'll know one day, if you have a child of your own. If that happens, you'll understand that there is nothing a mother won't do for her child. Absolutely nothing."

It hit me that perhaps one of the things she'd done was to end her affair with Ted back in the day. If she'd kept up her involvement with him, the stigma of how she'd broken up his marriage would have followed her for years, and would have affected their children, too.

Mom had never said anything like that to me before. I'd never known her to be so passionate—especially about anything to do with me. It was really nice.

"Anything, Haley. I'd do anything." Mom grinned. "Even if it caused me to break a nail."

She giggled and I giggled. Then we hugged.

"I have so many urgent matters to attend to today," Mom said, springing off of the sofa. "I have to get my hair done, of course, and I could use a fresh pedi. My goodness, my day is suddenly packed."

Mom was back to being Mom again, which I was totally cool with.

"Later," I called and left the house.

As I climbed into my Honda, I considered going back inside and telling Mom where she could find Ted. But then I thought better of it. Maybe she'd rather remember him as he was, back in the day when he was young, healthy, and vital.

I decided, too, that whatever had gone on in the past between my parents was their business, not mine. I was staying out of it.

But my heart ached a little for Mom. I wondered what other burdens she might have carried all these years.

With that ache came thoughts of Ty.

Would part of my heart always belong to him? Would I look back on my decision to forget about him and, one day, wonder *what if*?

I sat there in my car for a few minutes, thinking. Maybe I should call Amber and ask if she'd heard from Ty.

I grabbed my cell phone.

I scrolled through my contact list.

I called Liam instead.

When I rolled into the Holt's parking lot a little later, I was pleased to see that the crew I'd hired was already at work. From the quick look I got, everything seemed to be on schedule. The festival area had been blocked off, booths were being set up, and construction on the runway for the fashion show was moving along quickly.

I grabbed my things and got out of the car. I hoped I'd see Detective Shuman's plain vanilla cop-mobile. He'd promised he would interview Carrie today, and I really wanted him to get to it this morning.

Everybody would breathe easier when Asha's murder was solved.

Shuman's car was nowhere to be seen, so I headed into the store. If he didn't show up soon, I'd give him a call.

Checking in with Jeanette was my first priority—but it would be for her benefit, not mine. She'd want a status report on progress. I'd already spoken with Elise in marketing on the drive here and given her an update.

There was a lot of hand-holding involved with being an event planner.

When I got inside of Holt's, two of the checkout lanes were open and a few customers were in line. I'd seen the advertising blitz that had gone out announcing the festival that would begin tomorrow, compete with deep discounts and the special sales, so I wasn't surprised the store was so empty this morning.

As I headed for the breakroom to stow my handbag—a fabulous Marc Jacobs—Bella hurried out of the women's clothing department and cut me off.

"You want to hear some b.s.?" she demanded.

I always wanted to hear some b.s.

But from the look on her face, I knew this wasn't ordinary, run-of-the-mill, b.s.

"What's wrong?" I asked.

"Sandy. That sorry, no-good idiot of a boyfriend of hers."

"Oh my God. Last night was her big birthday dinner," I said.

"Nope," Bella said. "It was a total bust."

Oh, crap.

Chapter 26

"What happened?" I asked, as I hurried into the breakroom, Bella on my heels.

"I don't know."

At the lockers, I grabbed my cell phone and shoved my handbag inside.

"Did they have a fight?" I asked.

"I don't know."

I was starting to get slightly annoyed. I was worried about my friend, and *this close* to finding out what was wrong, but not getting anywhere.

"Then how do you know something happened?" I asked, closing my locker.

Bella huffed. "Sandy's not saying anything—except that everything was all right. It was fine. It was good. You know, that same b.s. she always says when anything comes up about that jackass boyfriend of hers."

Okay, now I understood.

"Let's go talk to her," I said.

I had festival prep to oversee, Jeanette to brief, Detective Shuman arriving any minute to interview a murder suspect, a team of investigative journalists with a multimillion-plus television audience on the way, the fate of the entire Holt's shopping center hanging in the balance, and my every action today likely to be under a microscope.

Well, all of that could wait. My friend was upset and I needed to find out what was going on.

Bella and I left the breakroom and found Sandy stocking coffeemakers in the housewares department.

"How'd it go last night?" I asked, and managed to sound somewhat pleasant.

"It was fine," Sandy said. "You know, okay. Good."

"But . . . ?"

She shrugged and said, "Well, you know, the evening didn't turn out exactly like I'd pictured."

"What did he do?" Bella demanded.

Sandy paused for a few seconds, then said, "He had to work. He couldn't help it. It was an emergency."

"Somebody needed an emergency tattoo?" I might have said that kind of loud.

"He did the best he could," Sandy insisted. "He ordered a pizza and had it delivered to my house."

"That's it?" Bella asked.

"He called me," Sandy added.

Oh my God. I hated that boyfriend of hers. She deserved so much better.

Bella looked like she might actually explode and said, "That's it? That's what he did for your birthday?"

"He said he'd make it up to me," Sandy insisted. "And he will. He's taking me out next weekend. He promised."

"That sounds like some b.s. to me," Bella grumbled.

"When you're in a relationship, you have to learn to compromise," Sandy said. "Things can't always be the way you want them."

"Why not?" Bella demanded.

"They just can't. It's give and take," Sandy said, then paused for a few seconds. "It would have been nice to go out for my birthday. But I understand, and I'm okay with what happened."

I wasn't okay with it, and I knew Bella wasn't either.

Sandy started unloading coffeemakers again, and Bella and I walked away.

"It's not right," Bella said. "I don't care what Sandy says, it's not right."

"I know, but what can we—"

My brain jumped into event-planner mode.

"Let's have a birthday party for her here," I said. "I'll run to the bakery and get a cake. You spread the word, and we'll surprise her."

"I like it," Bella said. "All right, let's do it."

I hurried to the breakroom, got cash from my wallet, and left the store. I knew Carrie had been swamped with all the baking she had to do for the festival, but I was confident she'd have a suitable cake and could whip out a happy birthday message in icing while I waited.

Unless—

I scanned the parking lot. Still no sign of Shuman. Whew! No way did I want him arresting Carrie and carting her away in handcuffs before I got Sandy's birthday cake.

Then someone else caught my eye.

Jack stood at the edge of the parking lot, watching the work crew and holding his cell phone to his ear. He looked hot, of course, dressed in jeans, a dark brown sweater, and CAT boots.

I'd known he would be here. He had a team providing security for the festival, so scoping out the setup today was essential.

He spotted me, ended his call, then joined me on the sidewalk.

When it came to his job, Jack was all business. We exchanged a quick greeting, then he got down to it, confirming that everything I'd asked for, and everything he'd recommended for the festival, was on schedule, moving forward, with no problems in sight.

"How's it looking here?" Jack asked.

"Shaping up as planned," I told him. "We're expecting a big crowd tomorrow, lots of kids, families."

"My team will be invisible," he assured me.

"The whole situation is about to change," I said.

He sensed something was up, so he moved in close and leaned down a little.

"I figured out who killed Asha," I whispered.

Jack looked surprised.

Cool.

I explained to him that I'd determined Carrie was the murderer and had been pushed to commit the crime because of Asha's probable threat to write another damning review if Carrie didn't pony up some big advertising bucks.

"Carrie is devoted to her bakery. Anybody who runs a business feels that way," I said. "She wasn't going to stand by and let Asha ruin it for her."

"What about evidence?" Jack asked.

Jeez, what was up with all the where's-the-evidence talk? Shuman had asked the same thing.

"It's in Asha's computer," I told him. "Shuman is having it analyzed. He'll be here later today to interview Carrie again, and arrest her."

Jack made no comment.

How come nobody—but me—was awed by my super sleuthing skills?

"Keep me posted," he said.

Jack headed for the parking lot again, and I went to the bakery.

The place smelled as delightful as ever. The display cases were jammed with an array of cookies, brownies, and beautifully decorated cupcakes. On the counter sat jars of colorful candies. There were no customers, but I spotted two girls I hadn't seen before wearing Cakes By Carrie aprons. Apparently, Carrie had brought in extra help to handle the workload.

I felt kind of bad being there, seeing how hard

Carrie had worked for the festival and knowing she was about to get hauled away in cuffs inside a squad car. But what else could I do? I needed a birthday cake for Sandy.

When I reached the counter, one of the new girls came over.

"I know you're super busy this morning, but I really need a birthday cake," I said. "Can you help me out?"

"Hang on a second," she said, and disappeared into the kitchen behind her.

A few seconds later, Carrie leaned around the doorway. She spotted me, and her expression soured a bit.

"Hi, Carrie," I called in my best please-like-me-and-do-what-I-ask voice. "I wouldn't ask for this when you're so busy if it wasn't important."

"All I've got is a vanilla quarter-sheet with buttercream icing," she said.

"That will be great," I told her. "Can you put a birthday message on it?"

She huffed and said, "Yeah, I guess."

The other clerk grabbed an order form and pen. "What do you want on the cake?"

"Would you put 'Happy birthday, Sandy' on it? Pink icing would be great, and maybe scatter some sugar confetti on it—"

Dena walked out of the kitchen. I hadn't seen her back there with Carrie. She gave me a big smile and said, "I've gotten all kinds of great comments from my customers. They're all excited about the festival."

"Good to know," I said.

She nodded toward her craft store next door and said, "I'd better get over there. Tons to do before tomorrow."

"Sure," I said. "If anything comes up, any problems, just—"

"Mom?"

Dena whipped around. Carrie stood in the kitchen doorway.

I got a weird feeling

"Don't forget we're making the bank run together this afternoon," Carrie said. "You said to remind you."

"Oh, yes, of course," Dena said, nodding.

"You're mother and daughter?" I asked, looking back and forth between them.

"We are," Dena said, giving me her biggest smile yet.

My weird feeling got weirder.

"I didn't know," I said.

Dena kept staring at me, her smile firmly in place, then said, "I've really got to run."

She didn't wait for me to say anything, just hurried out the door. When I turned around, Carrie had vanished.

"Here you go." The clerk showed me the cake she'd decorated with Sandy's birthday message, then sealed it in a pink bakery box.

"Thanks," I said.

I paid her and left the store.

As I headed to Holt's, my something's-weird feeling grew larger inside me.

I hadn't known that Dena was Carrie's mom. I'd had no idea, but why would I have? They had different last names. But that wasn't unusual, wasn't completely out-there. So why was it hitting me so hard?

Mom flashed in my head. How would she feel seeing me handcuffed and taken away by the police, as Dena would later today after Shuman interviewed Carrie? Nobody wanted to see that happen to her child.

Maybe that's why the whole mother-daughter revelation bothered me so much. I'd talked to Mom this morning. We'd connected in a way we seldom did. She'd told me that, despite our differences, she'd always be there for me—which was really great to hear.

But it was surprising, too. She'd said it with such passion. Her I'm-your-mother instincts seemed to have kicked in, and I knew she'd meant what she said.

Mom could be wrapped up in her own world at times—well, most of the time—so it was nice to hear that she was just like every other mom who'd do anything for her child—

Oh, crap.

I froze on the sidewalk, then whirled around and stared at the bakery and craft store, side by side, both of them owned by a mother-daughter combo.

A mother who, like all mothers, would do anything for her child.

And a daughter who, I suspected, had needed something big done for her.

Oh my God.

I was wrong.

Chapter 27

My brain was buzzing like crazy as I put the birthday cake in the breakroom refrigerator at Holt's. All I could think was that I'd been wrong.

Carrie hadn't murdered Asha—though she'd probably wanted to. Dena, her mom, had done it.

I was sure I was right this time.

But I had been sure yesterday when I'd told Shuman my oh-so brilliant theory and insisted he check out Asha's computer and show up here today to arrest Carrie.

No way could I be wrong again.

I dashed off a text message to Bella, letting her know we'd have the party later this afternoon, and hurried out of the breakroom.

I couldn't bring myself to call Shuman, backpedal, and insist he listen to my I-know-who-did-it-and-this-time-I'm-right idea. I needed to find some evidence. Something concrete that would prove Dena had shot and killed Asha.

I could think of only one place to find it.

I left Holt's and headed down the sidewalk toward the craft store. I spotted Jack on the other side of the parking lot, talking to two guys who I figured were from his security team.

For a few seconds I thought about bringing Jack in on this, letting him know that I'd learned Dena and Carrie were mother and daughter and that I knew—okay, strongly suspected—the true circumstances surrounding Asha's murder. But I'd already shot off my mouth to Jack. I didn't want to be wrong in front of him again.

Dena was outside her store; the door was propped open. She'd rolled several sets of display shelves onto the sidewalk and was busy moving merchandise onto them from a smaller version of a Holt's U-boat.

I had to play this carefully—I wasn't exactly known for my subtlety or finesse.

What I needed was evidence, so I had to get inside Dena's store and find it, somehow, without giving her the idea that I suspected her of anything. After all, she owned a gun and had already shot her husband. If I was right, she'd shot Asha, too.

I doubted she'd think twice about shooting me.

"Hi, again," I said, stopping next to her.

She looked up, surprised. "Oh, hi."

I tried for an I-don't-really-suspect-you-of-murder smile, but wasn't sure I really pulled it off.

"We're having a little birthday party for one of the girls at Holt's. That's why I needed the cake from Carrie," I said. "So I wanted to pick up some party supplies. You know, balloons, streamers, some paper plates, that kind of thing."

"Sure," Dena said. "Let me show you what I have."

"No, no, you don't have to do that," I told her. "You're busy and I don't want to keep you from what you're doing. I'll find them."

I didn't give her a chance to say anything before I slipped past her into the store.

Two older women were in the scrapbooking section, loading a handbasket with supplies. I didn't see a sales clerk.

I made a big show of looking up and down at the merchandise, then glanced back at the entrance. Dena was focused on the displays. I hurried to the rear of the store to the door marked EMPLOYEES ONLY, and dashed inside.

The stockroom was a fraction of the size of the one at Holt's, with a dozen tall shelving units packed with all sorts of new merchandise waiting to be displayed. I made my way through them and spotted an office area with a desk, a chair, a computer, and a printer. Two tall filing cabinets bracketed the store's rear exit door, stacked high with binders and catalogs. Notices, bulletins, and flyers were pinned to a corkboard over the desk. Everything looked neat and tiny, well organized.

I had only a few minutes in there before Dena would likely realize I hadn't picked out party supplies yet and would come looking for me. I had to move fast.

Shuman had told me Dena had a permit to carry concealed so it was likely she kept the weapon on her, which meant it was here somewhere. I was positive it was the gun that had been used in Asha's murder. All I had to do was find it and call Shuman. I'd let him worry about search warrants, chain of custody, and LAPD's proper procedures for gathering evidence.

The two file cabinets looked like a great place to hide a gun. No way did I want to leave my fingerprints on anything, so I yanked my sleeve over my hand and pulled open the top drawer of one of the file cabinets. Inside were papers tucked neatly into files. Same with the second drawer, and the third.

I reached for the handle of the fourth drawer. Voices.

I froze. My heartbeat shot up.

Oh my God, what was I going to tell Dena if she walked in a caught me? How would I explain myself?

I swallowed hard and strained to listen.

The voices faded away. I figured it must have been the two women who'd been shopping in the scrapbooking section moving past the stockroom door.

Jeez, I really hope that's what it was.

I turned back to the file cabinets. Lots more drawers to go.

I grabbed another handle and it hit me—I was looking in the wrong place.

Dena had accidentally shot her husband when her pistol, inside her handbag, had gone off. She had a permit to carry a concealed weapon. If she'd shot Asha after a confrontation near the Holt's loading dock—likely an unplanned meeting—that meant Dena kept her gun with her all the time, inside her handbag.

I eyed the desk. In my office at L.A. Affairs, I always stowed my handbag in the large, bottom desk drawer. Keeping my fingers inside my sweater sleeve, I rolled the drawer open.

Inside was a non-designer handbag—which was disturbing enough—and among the jumble of Dena's personal items, tucked into a special strap, was a .38 handgun.

Oh my God, I'd found it.

I had to call Shuman. He had to get here right away—or maybe he was already here, interviewing Carrie.

I swung around and reached for my cell phone.

Dena stood between the shelving units.

Her gaze dropped to the open desk drawer, then bounced up to me again.

"You killed Asha," I said.

"You have no proof," she told me.

"Detective Shuman will be here any minute. He'll see your gun and do a ballistics test. It will show—"

Dena grabbed a large wicker basket from the shelving unit and heaved it at me. I batted it away, but she was right behind it and shoved me aside. I fell against one of the file cabinets and my flailing arm struck the other one. I spun around as she pulled the pistol from her handbag.

"What gun?" Dena asked, pointing it at me. "By the time anyone arrives, this thing will be long gone. Now, step away from the door."

No way was I letting her escape so she could destroy evidence.

I dropped my arms onto each of the file cabinets, blocking the door.

"You thought you could get away with murder," I said. "Again."

"You mean that man I was married to?" Dena uttered a disgusted grunt. "I was cleared of all charges."

"But you murdered him, didn't you?" I said.

"It was an unfortunate accident," she insisted, then smirked. "Unfortunate for him that I found out about his string of girlfriends."

Oh my God, she'd really killed her husband.

"So that made it easier for you to kill Asha," I said.

"Some people deserve to die," Dena said. "She tried to ruin my daughter's bakery—and just when things were starting to go well for us."

"Us?"

Dena lowered her voice, as if we were gossiping over lunch, and said, "Carrie was a difficult child, especially after I divorced her father. She was a difficult teenager, always with problems. I tried to deal with her, and I did the best I could, but things were strained between us—until I bought her that bakery."

"With your husband's life insurance?" I asked.

"She insisted it was the only thing that would make her happy. She wanted to own a bakery. I didn't have that kind of money until . . ." Dena paused. "Well, let's just say the timing was perfect."

"So, then, everything was going along fine?" I said.

"Yes, finally. Finally. Finally we were getting along. We were talking, making plans, discussing our businesses. Finally she was happy."

"Then Asha wrote that awful review."

Dena's expression darkened. "What a little sneak. Going to work at the bakery, pretending to be Carrie's friend, then stabbing her in the back."

I nodded to the door behind me and said, "You must have spotted Asha out back, having a smoke near the loading dock. You went down there and confronted her."

"I went there to talk," Dena insisted. "She'd been into the bakery the day before. Can you imagine the gall? Waltzing into Carrie's shop all friendly-like."

I knew that Asha had been in Holt's the day before she was murdered, when she'd had that argument with Valerie Roderick near the customer service booth. Asha had probably been there to shop, but I suspected she'd been at the shopping center for a very different reason.

"What did she want?" I asked, though I was pretty sure I already knew.

"She had the nerve—the nerve—to tell Carrie that if she wanted to be sure nothing bad was said about her bakery, she could take out an ad on her website."

Wow, I'd been right.

It wasn't much consolation, with Dena still pointing that gun at me.

"Do you have any idea how much money I had to pour into that bakery for advertising, special promotions, and discounted prices to make up for that awful review?" Dena demanded.

"Carrie agreed to pay for the ad?"

"What choice did she have?" Dena shook her head. "I couldn't go through that with Carrie again. I couldn't."

"Asha came back the next day to finalize the ad with Carrie," I said, which was a guess on my part, but it made sense. "You spotted her out back by the Dumpster."

"Oh, yes, there she was having a leisurely smoke, not at all concerned that she was about the ruin another business." Dena spit out the words as if they were bitter on her tongue, then paused and drew in a long breath. "I wanted to make sure that, after Carrie bought that ad, Asha didn't have any intentions of writing more lies about the bakery. And, of course, I wanted to tell Carrie she didn't have to worry about Asha ever again."

"How'd that work out?" I asked. I already knew the answer. I wanted to keep Dena talking until I could figure out how to get out of this mess.

Dena seemed to get lost in thought for a few

minutes, remembering, I figured, how it had gone down with Asha.

"She had no intention of settling for just one ad, right? It would never have ended," I said. "So you ended it."

"What else could I do?" she said. "Call the police? Take legal action? Wait for months, and all the while Asha's was still writing those horrible reviews?"

"You shot Asha."

Dena nodded slowly, then locked the gun in a two-handed grip and said, "And now, I'm going to have to shoot you, too."

I grabbed one of the binders from the top of the file cabinet and threw it at her. The gun went off. A bullet whizzed past my head.

No way was I giving her a chance to get off another shot.

I lurched forward and grabbed her arm, pushing it away. Dena whirled around, dragging me with her. I stumbled over the leg of the chair and hit the floor hard. Another shot rang out, this one burying into the desk.

I scrambled to my feet. Dena danced backwards, following my movement with the gun. I flung the chair at her, striking her in the knees, and jumped to the side.

"Put the gun down!"

Jack appeared among the shelving units. Dena swung the gun his way.

I threw myself at her, a full-body blow, knocking her down. We landed hard on the floor,

Dena facedown, me on top. I grabbed her wrists with both hands. Dena bucked and wiggled, trying to throw me off.

Just when I was considering grabbing a handful of her hair for a fight-ending face-plant, a CAT boot came down on Dena's gun hand. She screamed. I was jerked upward, off of her.

"I'll take it from here," Shuman said, letting go of me.

He whipped out handcuffs. Jack helped secured her wrists, then turned to me.

"Are you okay?" he asked.

No, I wasn't okay. My heart raced, my adrenaline pumped, and parts of me were in pain.

I guess Jack realized that because he pulled me close and wrapped both arms around me.

Okay, now I was better.

"How did you know something was wrong?" I asked, looking up at him.

"When I was in the parking lot I saw you walk into this place," Jack said. "I had a feeling something was up, so I came over. I heard the shots."

"I was next door talking to Carrie," Shuman said, looking angry. "You shouldn't have come in here alone, Haley. You shouldn't have put yourself in this dangerous position. What were you thinking?"

"You should have told me what you were doing," Jack said, sounding none too happy with me. "I was right outside. Right there in the parking lot. Why didn't you let me know?"

Jeez, I solved a murder, saved Jack from being shot, and this was the thanks I got?

I pushed away from Jack.

"Don't act like this is all my fault," I told them. "You two are the ones who insisted on having some evidence."

That shut them up.

"Clean up this mess," I said, waving my arms around. "I have a birthday party to go to."

I left.

Chapter 28

"Everything is wonderful, Haley, just wonderful," Jeanette said.

"Thank you," I said, and managed to sound humble, even though I knew I'd done a great job staging the festival.

We were standing in the Holt's parking lot, just outside the spacious white tent I'd had erected for VIPs. Executives from the corporate office, the team of investigative journalists, and the shop owners were inside, taking advantage of the comfy seating groups to chat.

"Actually," Jeanette said, "everything is spectacular."

I'd arranged for one of L.A.s finest caterers to provide food for the VIPs, and had included a full bar—which, as always, added to the *spectacular* occasion.

Nearby, the festival was winding down. Folks

had crowded the area all day, eating, enjoying the games, moving through the stores to shop, and returning to the festival again.

I spotted Jack making his way past the kids' area. He and his team had been on the go all day. So far, there hadn't been one minute of trouble.

"Those journalists are a little disappointed," Jeanette whispered, then smiled. "With the murder solved, an arrest made, and the festival going so well, they don't have much to report. The police closing the case yesterday was certainly a lucky break for us."

"It was," I agreed, though, really, it was all me.

I hadn't heard from Shuman since he'd left the craft store with Dena in handcuffs. I knew he was busy. I figured he'd get clear soon and fill me in on everything.

My cell phone rang. Jeanette headed back into the VIP tent while I answered.

"Ms. Randolph, this is Kendal from Nuovo. I have some good news."

A little more good news today wouldn't hurt.

"Your two Mystique clutch bags have arrived," she said.

I allowed myself a little fist pump and said, "Great. Thanks."

Of course, I wanted to rush right over—really, you can never get your hands on a fabulous bag too soon.

After the last few days, I decided to treat myself. I could pick up Marcie, go to Nuovo, bask in the glory of our Mystiques, and get back here in time to make sure everything was handled when the festival officially closed.

"I'll pick them up later today," I said.

"Very well. I'll see you then."

"Great—oh, wait," I said. "What about Chandra? She's my personal shopper there."

Kendal paused for only a second or two and said, "Chandra has moved on to accept new opportunities."

I wondered if "accept new opportunities" was code for "got fired," or maybe "quit without notice."

Either way, not my problem.

"Okay, see you later," I said, and ended the call.

I dashed off a text message to Marcie telling her to meet me at my apartment so we could pick up our Mystiques. She immediately texted back a dozen happy faces.

As I was heading back into the VIP tent, I caught sight of Shuman getting out of his car. I walked over to meet him.

"Are you feeling okay?" he asked, looking concerned. "You took a couple of hard hits yesterday."

I had some bruises from wrestling around with Dena, but nothing permanent.

"I'm good," I said. "What's up with Dena?"

"Ballistics matched her gun with the murder weapon," Shuman said. "Looks like she's in for a long prison sentence."

I gazed across the parking lot. The craft store

was closed, but the bakery was doing a brisk business.

Of course, I could never go in there again. Carrie, no doubt, blamed me for her mom's arrest. I wondered how long she could keep the bakery going without Dena's help.

"Do you think Carrie was involved with Asha's murder?" I asked.

When I'd been in her bakery and told her about Asha's death, Carrie had gone completely whacko. She must have suspected her mom was behind the murder.

Shuman shrugged. "Dena claims not, but I don't know. Maybe."

Even if Carrie was involved, I knew Dena would keep it a secret. It was a total mom thing to do.

I nodded to the VIP tent. "There's food, if you're hungry."

Shuman shook his head and grinned. "I've got a date tonight."

"Cool."

He left and I made a lap through the festival, making sure everything was still running smoothly with no problems, then checked on things in the VIP tent. No problems there, either.

Security announced that the festival was over and guided the remaining guests out of the area. I told Jeanette I had something to take care of with the construction crew—a total lie, but oh well—and left.

I drove to my apartment and hurried inside.

Marcie would be here in a bit, but no way was I going to Nuovo dressed in the L.A. Affairs standard uniform of black pants and sweater—even though it was an upgraded version and I looked totally hot in it.

When I got to my bedroom, my doorbell rang. Wow, Marcie was really early. She must be more excited than me to get our Mystiques. Maybe we'd find something totally cool to wear with them at Nuovo—or maybe I'd find something totally hot to wear on my romantic weekend with Liam.

I hurried to the front door and yanked it open.

Ty stood outside.

I couldn't move. I couldn't speak. I couldn't seem to comprehend that he was standing in front of me.

He had on jeans and a polo shirt. His hair brushed his collar. He had a short beard.

And he looked handsome.

My heart pounded so hard I could hear it in my ears.

"Can I come in?" he asked.

I couldn't form any words. I stepped back and he walked into my living room.

"I just got back," he said. "Right now. This minute. I came straight here."

All I could do was look at him.

"I've had a lot of time to think," he said. "That's why I left, you know. I had to sort things through, figure out . . . figure out my life. And I've done that."

Ty stepped closer and said, "I'm in love with you, Haley."

My mouth fell open. I blinked twice to make sure I was really seeing him, that this wasn't some sort of weird hallucination.

"You—you *what*?" I managed to ask.

"I love you."

Oh, crap.